GHOST HOUSE

On holiday, Michael Wayland and his wife like the look of an empty house in a place called Bracken Bottom and decide to buy it. However, known as 'Ghost House', it has a sullied past — the previous owner was hanged for murder. Then, when Michael and his wife move in, odd things happen. A creaking gate is mysteriously oiled. And who is the strange man on the motorcycle — what is the message being flashed in the wood at night?

Books by Gerald Verner
in the Linford Mystery Library:

THE LAST WARNING
DENE OF THE SECRET SERVICE
THE NURSERY RHYME MURDERS
TERROR TOWER
THE CLEVERNESS OF MR. BUDD
THE SEVEN LAMPS
THEY WALK IN DARKNESS
THE HEEL OF ACHILLES
DEAD SECRET
MR. BUDD STEPS IN
THE RETURN OF MR. BUDD
MR. BUDD AGAIN
QUEER FACE
THE CRIMSON RAMBLERS

0135920827

SPECIAL MESSAGE TO READERS

This book is published under the auspices of

THE ULVERSCROFT FOUNDATION

(registered charity No. 264873 UK)

Established in 1972 to provide funds for research, diagnosis and treatment of eye diseases. Examples of contributions made are: —

A Children's Assessment Unit at Moorfield's Hospital, London.

•

Twin operating theatres at the Western Ophthalmic Hospital, London.

•

A Chair of Ophthalmology at the Royal Australian College of Ophthalmologists.

•

The Ulverscroft Children's Eye Unit at the Great Ormond Street Hospital For Sick Children, London.

You can help further the work of the Foundation by making a donation or leaving a legacy. Every contribution, no matter how small, is received with gratitude. Please write for details to:

THE ULVERSCROFT FOUNDATION,
The Green, Bradgate Road, Anstey,
Leicester LE7 7FU, England.
Telephone: (0116) 236 4325

In Australia write to:

THE ULVERSCROFT FOUNDATION,
c/o The Royal Australian and New Zealand
College of Ophthalmologists,
94-98 Chalmers Street, Surry Hills,
N.S.W. 2010, Australia

GERALD VERNER

GHOST HOUSE

Complete and Unabridged

LINFORD
Leicester

First published in Great Britain

First Linford Edition
published 2012

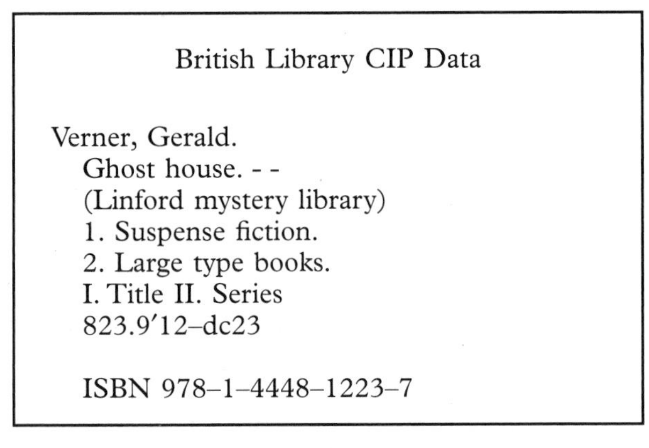
British Library CIP Data

Verner, Gerald.
Ghost house. - -
(Linford mystery library)
1. Suspense fiction.
2. Large type books.
I. Title II. Series
823.9′12–dc23

ISBN 978–1–4448–1223–7

Published by
F. A. Thorpe (Publishing)
Anstey, Leicestershire

Set by Words & Graphics Ltd.
Anstey, Leicestershire
Printed and bound in Great Britain by
T. J. International Ltd., Padstow, Cornwall

This book is printed on acid-free paper

1

For some time Ann Wayland had been feeling uneasy.

Every now and again she gave her husband a quick, sidelong glance and opened her mouth to speak, but she thought better of it and remained silent.

But she was definitely uneasy.

Michael Wayland appeared quite unconcerned as he sat behind the wheel of the little car, a cigarette drooping from his lips, his eyes on the narrow road ahead. But there were certain signs that told Ann he was not quite so unconcerned as he looked. A very slight pucker between the brows; a twitch now and again to his nostrils — sure evidence, to anyone who knew him intimately, that he was worried.

The road down which they were travelling was getting narrower and more deeply rutted; the high banks on either side, surmounted by straggling hedges and trees, were getting higher and higher, so that it was like driving through a cutting.

At last she could keep silent no longer. She said:

'Michael.'

'Yes, darling?' he answered, without turning his head.

'Where are we?'

A wry smile twisted his mobile mouth.

'To be quite candid, I haven't the faintest idea,' he said.

'You said — ' began Ann.

'I know,' he broke in, 'but I said it five miles back. I rather think we took the wrong turning at the crossroads. There wasn't a signpost . . . '

'Why didn't you look at the map?' she asked.

'I was relying on what that man told me at the hotel in Camsford,' answered Michael. '*He* said it was the left-hand road . . . '

'It isn't going to be a road at all much longer,' she remarked. 'It's getting narrower and narrower . . . '

'You sound like Alice in Wonderland,'

grinned Michael.

'I feel rather like it,' she retorted. 'I think you'd better turn back.'

'That's easier said than done,' he answered. 'How can I? There isn't room to turn the car.'

'Can't you back it, or something . . . ?'

'Not for nearly two miles, darling,' he said.

'Then what are we going to do?' she demanded.

'Go on — that's all we can do,' he answered. 'This must lead somewhere.'

'We were supposed to be going to West Dittersham, remember?' said Ann.

'There's no reason why we should go to West Dittersham, is there?' inquired her husband,

'Well, that's where you said we were going,' she replied.

Michael grinned.

'One of the joys of a motor tour,' he remarked easily, 'is that you are not restricted to any fixed programme. You can roam about just where the fancy takes you . . . '

'Or the mistakes of the driver,' put in

Ann mischievously.

'That's unkind,' said Michael. 'I was quite sure that that man at the hotel knew what he was talking about . . . '

'And the result is that we're landed in a mess,' she finished.

'You never know,' he said. 'We may have cause to be grateful to him, after all.'

'And we may not,' said Ann.

'West Dittersham might not have been all it's cracked up to be,' he said hopefully. 'Perhaps we shall come across something better.'

He was driving quite slowly and, as they rounded a bend in the road, he saw in front of them a gate. The road suddenly narrowed, and the gate barred all further progress.

'That's the end of the road,' said Ann as Michael slowed and brought the car to a stop. 'You'll have to go back now.'

'We may as well see what's beyond the gate,' he said, as he opened the door of the car and slid out from behind the wheel.

'I was afraid we'd get stuck in a cul-de-sac, or something,' said Ann bitterly, as she followed.

'Well, it's hardly a cul-de-sac, so it must be something,' retorted her husband. 'We may be on the verge of discovering some lovely spot far from the vulgar crowd. Come on, and keep your fingers crossed.'

He led the way over to the gate. It was made of iron and was red with rust. As he opened it, it uttered a loud and protesting squeak.

'H'm,' remarked Michael. 'Those hinges haven't been oiled for some years. Now, let's see what's beyond.'

'I expect it leads to somebody's house,' said Ann.

They entered a weed-grown drive, lined on either side by overgrown bushes. It turned sharply a few yards farther on, and Michael, who was ahead, caught sight of a neglected garden and a house that stood in a screen of trees.

'There is a house,' he said, 'but I think it's empty . . . '

Ann uttered an exclamation as she joined him.

'Michael,' she exclaimed. 'What a

lovely little place.'

The house was low-built, with a red-tiled roof that was patched with green here and there, where the moss had grown. Over the porch a rambler rose grew in wild profusion and, on either side, were casement windows with leaded panes.

'Are you sure it's empty?' asked Ann, as she stood beside him and looked at the house with delight. 'It's really the sweetest little place,'

'There don't seem to be any curtains at any of the windows,' he said, 'and I shouldn't think, if there was anybody living there, they'd let the garden get into that state. Let's go and see.'

'Suppose there is somebody there?' she asked doubtfully.

'We can always explain that we took the wrong road,' he said. 'Come on.'

She followed him to the end of the short approach where it widened to a half circle before the porch. The weeds ran riot everywhere and long trails of brambles lay tangled over the path.

'Mind your ankles,' warned Michael.

'It's thick with nettles.'

There was no sign of life as they approached the front door with its overhanging porch. The paint was blistered and peeling, and the rambler had grown so thick and straggly that it was impossible to reach the door without carefully pulling its long, thorny stems aside.

'Not much doubt that it's empty,' remarked Michael, as they stood gazing at it. 'I wonder who it belongs to?'

'It's the nicest little house I've ever seen,' said Ann enthusiastically. 'If it was painted, and the garden tided up, it would be perfect.'

'I wonder why it's empty?' said Michael, frowning. 'I should have thought it would be snapped up quickly enough these days.'

'I don't suppose many people know there's a house here at all,' said Ann. 'It's completely hidden away from any main road, isn't it? Let's see if we can get in. I'd love to see what it's like inside.'

They went round to the back, picking their way carefully amid the rubbish and tangled undergrowth. A small veranda ran part of the length of the house at the rear, with french windows opening from one of the rooms on to it. These had evidently been put in more recently by some previous tenant, for they were modern in comparison to the rest of the building.

Ann ran up a shallow flight of four steps that led up to the veranda and peered in through the french windows.

'Michael,' she cried in delight, 'come and look! It's all oak panelling and old beams. It's beautiful . . . '

But Michael was exploring round some outhouses that were built on to the side of the house. There was a small window, which looked as if it might belong to a pantry, beside one of these, and he saw that one of the small diamond-shaped panes was broken near the latch. Removing a sharp splinter of glass, he managed to get his hand inside. Fumbling about, he found the old-fashioned latch, and the next moment had the window open.

He called to Ann, and she came quickly.

'I think I can wriggle through that,' he

said, pointing to the small window. 'If I can, I can go round and open the door for you.'

He gripped the sill and hauled himself up. The window was very narrow and he almost stuck halfway, but he managed it, and found himself, as he had expected, in a small pantry.

'Go round to the front,' he said, looking out at Ann. 'I'll have the door open in a couple of shakes.'

Everything was thick with dust and draped in cobwebs. It was evident that it was a long time since the place had been occupied. Michael made his way through a kitchen, along a short passage by the side of a staircase to a wide, square hall. Through the glass of a narrow window beside the oaken front door, he could see Ann pulling aside the rambler rose.

He had some difficulty with the bolts fastening the door, they had rusted badly in their sockets, but he managed at last to pull them back, and opened the door.

'How are you, Mrs. Wayland?' he greeted with an elaborate bow. 'So nice of you to call. *Do* come in.'

She came in quickly, looking about her with interest.

'Oh,' she said, as she caught sight of the staircase. 'Do look, Michael. What a lovely staircase — all carved, solid oak . . . '

'Old oak too,' said Michael. 'There's no stain on that. Black from sheer age.'

'And the front door,' said Ann. 'What a shame to have painted the outside . . . '

She opened a door to the right of the square hall and peered into the room beyond.

'This is the room that opens on to the veranda,' she called. 'It's quite big . . . Oh, it *is* a lovely house . . . '

There was another room on the opposite side, a room that must have been the drawing room, for an expensive paper of white and gold was peeling off the walls. The white was dirty, and the gold going black, but it had been a very good paper.

They explored upstairs. There were three bedrooms and a rather well-fitted bathroom, much more modern than the house itself, although, like everything else, it was covered with grime and cobwebs. Two of the bedrooms were fairly large, the third was smaller.

Ann was clearly enchanted with everything she saw.

'It could be made beautiful, Michael,' she said, when they finished up in the kitchen, a long, low room with an old-fashioned dresser and a range that was broken and rusty. 'If it was cleaned and painted . . . '

'It is rather nice,' he agreed.

'It's charming,' she said. She looked at him questioningly. 'I wish we could have it, Michael. It's just the place we've been looking for . . . '

'Don't you think it's a little — well, remote?' he said doubtfully.

'But that's its greatest charm,' answered Ann. 'We've always got the flat in town if we get tired of solitude. The garden could be made to look really delightful, and that room upstairs would make you a lovely study where you could write without any distraction . . . Do let's try and get it, darling . . . '

'We've got to find out who it belongs to first,' said Michael. 'I must say I like it myself . . . '

'There must be somebody who knows who it belongs to,' said Ann. 'Let's see if we can find a village, or something, where we can inquire.'

'We've got to get out of that wretched lane before we can go anywhere,' said Michael. The line in his forehead deepened as he thought. 'I've got it,' he exclaimed. 'I'll drive in and turn the car round in front of the house. I wonder what it's called, by the way?'

But although they looked carefully there was neither name nor number.

While Ann waited for him outside, Michael carefully bolted the front door and made his way out through the pantry window.

'I suppose,' he said as he joined his wife, 'that we could be had up for breaking and entering. If you'll hold the gate open, I'll drive the car in.'

He succeeded in turning the car on the semicircle in front of the porch. Ann got in and he drove out, stopping when he was through the gate, to return and fasten it.

'Now,' he said, as he drove back up the lane, 'we'd better make for the cross-roads . . . '

When they reached the crossroads, Michael stopped the car and frowned.

'Which way shall we go?' he asked. 'I've no idea where any of 'em lead to.'

'Let's try the right-hand one this time,' said Ann. 'That man at the hotel probably meant the right-hand one when he said the left.'

'Probably he was ambidextrous,' grinned Michael.

Whatever he'd been, Ann proved to be right in her choice. After a short distance they came to the beginning of a village, and presently were gently running up an old-fashioned High Street. There were the usual collection of small shops, a public house, a small bank, a teashop of the 'Olde Worlde' type, and, almost at the top, an estate agents.

'Let's try there,' suggested Ann. 'They ought to know something about the house.'

Michael nodded.

'We can but try,' he said, and pulled the car up outside the small, bow-fronted house, which bore across its fascia the name 'Cobb and Yardle' with the qualifying statement beneath: 'Auctioneers and Estate Agents'.

In a small outer office they found a sleepy-looking clerk reading a rather lurid-covered book which he hastily put away as they came in.

'Good afternoon,' said Michael. 'I want to make an inquiry concerning a house . . . '

'Yes, sir,' the clerk said with alacrity, before he could get any further. 'You mean The Croft in Amstell Road. A very fine property, sir, covering twenty-six acres — '

'I don't mean The Croft at all,' broke in Michael. 'I mean a period cottage that lies at the end of a narrow lane leading up to the crossroads . . . '

The clerk, who was quite a youth — he couldn't have been more than eighteen or nineteen — screwed up his face.

'I don't think I know the property, sir,'

he said, shaking his head.

'It's a very old house,' put in Ann. 'It hadn't any name that we could see.'

The clerk still appeared puzzled.

'The road that dips steeply into a sort of hollow,' explained Michael. 'It's the left-hand road as you come from Camsford. There's an iron gate at the end of it that leads to the house we mean.'

The clerk shook his head again.

'I've no recollection of it at all, sir,' he said. 'Had it got one of our boards on it?'

'It hadn't any board at all,' said Michael. 'But it's empty, and it appears to have been empty for some years, by the look of it.'

'You must know the place,' said Ann. 'It's a low house, built of old red brick, with a veranda at the back . . . '

But quite obviously the clerk did not know it.

'I'm afraid I can't help you,' he said. 'If you'll wait for a moment, I'll have a word with Mr. Yardle.'

He got up and went through a door at the back of the office.

'They don't seem to know anything

about it,' remarked Michael in a low voice, when he had gone.

'Perhaps it's such a long time since anyone has inquired about it, that they've forgotten it's there,' suggested Ann.

'Maybe,' he agreed. 'Like a cigarette, darling?'

She shook her head.

'No thanks,' she said. 'I'd love some tea, though.'

Michael lit his own cigarette.

'We'll get some as soon as we've finished here. There was a place down the road . . . '

The clerk came back.

'Will you come in, please,' he said.

They followed him into a larger and more comfortably furnished office. Behind a big untidy writing-table sat a stout, red-faced man with a pleasant smile. He rose as they came in and extended a hand across the table.

'Sit down, Mr. . . . ?' he paused.

'Wayland — Michael Wayland,' said Michael. 'This is my wife.'

'How do you do, Mrs. Wayland?' said the genial Mr. Yardle. 'Please sit down.

Now, how can I help you?'

Michael explained all over again. Obviously the clerk had not been very clear.

'The only place I can think of that answers your description, Mr. Wayland,' said the estate agent thoughtfully, 'is Bracken Cottage. That's at the end of a long lane that leads nowhere else.'

'That sounds like the place,' said Michael. 'Can you tell me who it belongs to?'

Mr. Yardle hesitated. Picking up a pencil he rolled it gently up and down his blotting-pad. There was, thought Michael, a rather queer expression on his florid face.

'What is your object in making these inquiries?' he asked, after a slight pause.

Michael looked mildly surprised.

'I am interested in buying it, if the price is right,' he answered.

'I don't know whether that would be possible,' said Mr. Yardle. 'I couldn't say whether it's for sale.'

'I suppose it would be possible to find that out from the owner,' suggested

Michael a little irritably.

'The owner is dead,' answered Mr. Yardle shortly. The genial expression had faded from his face and he looked worried. 'I should strongly advise you, Mr. — er — Wayland, to give up the idea of that particular property. If you wish to settle in this district, and it's a charming locality, a charming locality, we have a number of very suitable houses on our books . . . '

'I'm not interested in any other houses,' cut in Michael curtly. 'If you are not prepared to help me any further, we may as well go . . . '

'Have you ever heard of William Crayle?' interrupted the estate agent.

'William Crayle?' repeated Michael. The name seemed familiar, but he couldn't remember why. 'No, I can't recollect . . . '

'Was he the owner of Bracken Cottage?' asked Ann.

Mr. Yardle nodded soberly.

'He was,' he answered. 'I told you he was dead. Actually, he was hanged — for murder.'

2

Even as Mr. Yardle spoke, Michael Wayland remembered why the name of William Crayle had seemed so familiar. Five years ago the newspapers had been full of it in connection with the sensational trial in which Crayle had played the principal part.

'You mean the man who shot that fellow, what-was-his-name?' he exclaimed.

Mr. Yardle nodded slowly.

'Helman,' he said. 'That was the man's name. It was a particularly cold-blooded murder. I don't know whether you remember the details . . . ?'

'I read the newspaper reports at the time,' interrupted Michael, 'but I can't say I remember much about it — except the name. However, that doesn't matter. What I'm interested in is this house. It must belong to somebody . . . '

'It does.' The estate agent nodded again. 'It belongs to Crayle's sister, now.

She inherited everything as next of kin.'

'Do you think she would sell?' asked Michael.

'That I can't say,' answered Mr. Yardle cautiously. 'I believe at one time — soon after the — er — execution — it was put on the market, but nobody would buy it. I suppose its association with Crayle put people off.'

'But how silly,' interposed Ann. 'As if that made any difference to the house. Just because it belonged to a murderer doesn't alter the fact that it's a charming place . . . '

'It hasn't put you off, darling?' asked Michael.

'Of course not,' she declared. 'I don't care who it once belonged to.'

Mr. Yardle looked at her and pursed his lips.

'I think I ought to tell you that it has a very bad reputation in the district,' he said. 'Very few people would go near it — even in daylight — '

'I suppose they imagine it's haunted, or some such nonsense,' broke in Ann. 'Well, I'm not in the least superstitious and neither is my husband . . . '

'So it boils down to the question of whether this woman is willing to sell,' said Michael. 'I'm prepared to buy at a reasonable price — say two thousand to two thousand five hundred. Are you willing to act in the matter, or would you rather I arranged with some other firm?'

'I shall be delighted to act for you, Mr. Wayland, if you are determined to acquire the property,' said Mr. Yardle. 'Of course, I can't promise the present owner, Mrs. Newsome, will sell — '

'If she was willing to sell before,' interrupted Michael, 'I should think she'd be willing to now. You say it was put up for sale but — '

'Oh, yes,' said the estate agent. 'It was in the hands of Renward and Trotter of Camsford — Mrs. Newsome lives in Camsford. I shall be pleased to get in touch with her and find out what her attitude is.'

'I'd be much obliged if you would,' said Michael. He took his wallet from his breast pocket and selected a card. 'Here is my London address,' he continued, laying the card on the writing-table in front of the estate agent. 'My wife and I are on a motoring tour at present, but that will always find me . . . '

'Couldn't we call back here?' suggested Ann. 'How long do you think it will be, Mr. Yardle, before you hear from Mrs. Newsome?'

'That, of course, I can't say definitely,' replied Mr. Yardle, tapping gently on the blotting-pad with the point of his pencil. 'I shall write at once, but how long it will take before Mrs. Newsome replies . . . ' He shrugged his shoulders.

'Today is Wednesday,' said Ann. 'If we came back next Monday, you ought to have heard something.'

'Yes, I should say that would be possible,' agreed the estate agent.

'Then we'll leave it at that,' said Michael. 'You get in touch with Mrs. Newsome, and we'll call back on Monday. Now let's go and get some tea, darling.'

Mr. Yardle accompanied them through the outer office to the door and stood watching them as they got into the car. As he returned to his own office, he was frowning and there was a troubled expression on his genial face

Peg's Kitchen was the usual type of tearoom that can be found in any English village High Street. It was full of imitation old oak and laden with gleaming brass and copper. It was quite empty when Ann and Michael entered, and they selected a table comfortably placed in one corner. The table wobbled badly and none of the chair-legs appeared to be the same length, but, apart from that, it wasn't worse then any other place of its kind

A small, white-haired, elderly woman, in a flowered apron — presumably 'Peg' — came to take their order from behind a curtained recess at the back of the room. She was a pleasant little woman, although her face looked rather thin and careworn. Ann got the impression that Peg's Kitchen was not a very profitable business Michael ordered tea and cakes, leaned back in his chair, which required a considerable effort of balance, and lighted a cigarette.

'Well,' he said, 'I wonder what Mrs.

Newsome's answer will be?'

Ann rested her chin on her clasped hands, her elbows on the table.

'I hope it's 'yes',' she said.

'You've set your heart on that house, haven't you?' said Michael, smiling.

'I have,' she admitted. 'It could be made absolutely heavenly, Michael. I can just see it when I've finished with it.'

'I don't think Yardle is very happy about us having it,' said Michael. 'He did his best to put us off, didn't he?'

'He probably hoped we'd be interested in a more expensive property,' said Ann. 'That house with twenty-seven acres, or whatever it was . . . '

'I think you're wrong there,' said Michael, shaking his head. 'It's my opinion that he's firmly on the side of the local superstition — '

'How ridiculous,' she broke in. 'This man, what was his name?'

'Crayle,' said Michael.

'This man Crayle didn't commit the murder at the house, did he?'

'No,' answered Michael. 'As I told Yardle, I don't remember much about it, but I think he shot Helman from a car — in the road.'

'Like a gangster killing on the pictures,' exclaimed Ann. 'How exciting.'

'I believe it was something like that,' agreed Michael. 'I must ask Hoppy. He'll know all about it.'

Bob Hopkins, known to all his friends as 'Hoppy' was crime reporter on the *Daily Messenger*, and a great personal friend of both Michael and Ann's.

The white-haired woman brought the tea and set it down in front of Ann. It was really hot and neither too strong nor too weak. The cakes, obviously home-made looked delicious. As Ann was pouring out the tea there came the sound of a motorbike from outside. Looking towards the window, Michael saw a rakish, red-painted motorcycle draw into the kerb opposite the door and stop.

The rider, a small man in a leather jacket and a white crash helmet, swung himself out of the saddle, propped up the machine, and entered the teashop.

The elderly proprietress came out from behind the screening curtain as he removed the crash helmet, revealing a thin face with very smooth dark hair that shone with an excess of brilliantine.

'Afternoon,' he said in a pronounced cockney twang. 'Can I 'ave some tea? I'd like a coupla poached eggs on toast, Ma, if yer can do 'em, lot's o' bread and butter an' jam, an' some cikes.'

She nodded and disappeared again behind the curtain. The newcomer went over to a table, in the other corner to the one occupied by Ann and Michael, sat down, pulled out a packet of Woodbines, extracted a cigarette, stuck it in his mouth, and lit it with a large lighter. Blowing out a cloud of smoke, he looked round the teashop with an inquisitive expression. He wasn't very old — Michael guessed him to be about thirty-six — but his face was wrinkled like a monkey's. His small, bright eyes, not unlike a monkey's, either, were set a trifle too near his longish nose. The lower lip of his mouth protruded, pulling down the corners, and giving to his face a rather bad-tempered expression.

'These cakes are really lovely,' said

Ann, helping herself to another. 'Try those pinky ones, Michael.'

Michael took a 'pinky one'.

'H'm, quite nice,' he said. 'Nearly as nice as the ones you make yourself.'

'I'll tell you something,' said Ann, as she poured out more tea, 'when we get to Bracken Cottage, we'll have to have the kitchen modernized. Nobody could possibly cook anything in the place as it is.'

Michael happened to be looking at the newcomer while she was speaking. At the words 'Bracken Cottage' a sudden change came over the thin face. The close-set eyes narrowed to mere slits and the protruding underlip was drawn in. He looked as if he had suddenly held his breath and his whole body had become tense.

He caught sight of Michael looking at him and almost instantly relaxed. With an elaborate, and totally unconvincing yawn, he stubbed out his half-smoked cigarette in a plate and immediately took out another and lit it.

But there was no doubt that Ann's words had given him a shock.

Michael wondered why.

What could this little cockney know about the cottage?

Probably nothing. It might be that he remembered the trial and associated Bracken Cottage with Crayle. That was the most likely explanation. He looked the kind of fellow who would take an interest in that sort of thing . . .

'What's the matter with you, Michael?' Ann's voice broke in on his thoughts. 'I've asked you twice for a cigarette.'

'I'm terribly sorry, darling,' apologized her husband. 'I was thinking . . . '

He took out his case and held it out to her. She took a cigarette and he lighted it for her. Through the smoke he saw that she was eyeing him curiously.

At that moment the proprietress of the establishment reappeared through the curtain with a laden tray, which she took over and set down in front of the man in the leather jacket. While she was busy removing the various items from the tray, Ann leaned forward and whispered;

'Michael, why do you keep staring at that man?'

'I was interested to see the effect it had on him when you mentioned Bracken Cottage,' he answered.

'The effect?' she repeated, frowning. 'What do you mean?'

Michael told her, keeping his voice low enough not to be heard by the other.

'How extraordinary,' said Ann. 'Perhaps he lives round here?'

Michael shook his head.

'I shouldn't think so,' he said. 'He looks to me like a typical London East-Ender.'

The white-haired woman came over to their table and inquired if they wanted anything else.

'No, thanks,' said Ann. 'We thoroughly enjoyed your cakes.'

The elderly woman looked pleased.

'I'm rather fond of making pastry,' she said. 'The difficulty is to know how much to make. Cakes are not nice unless they're eaten fresh.'

'Do you get many people in here?' asked Michael.

She shook her head.

'Not as many as I'd like,' she replied. 'The morning coffee trade is fairly good

— people come in after they've done their shopping. But I don't get many for teas — not in the week. Sometimes at the weekends I'm busy. I open on Sundays.'

She wrote out the bill and laid it beside Michael's plate. He took a note from his wallet and handed it to her.

'I'll get you the change,' she said.

When she had retired behind the curtain, Michael said:

'I never quite know what to do about tips in these kind of places. It's all right when you're only dealing with a waitress . . . '

'Leave something under your plate,' said Ann. 'I'm sure she can do with everything she can get. The place can't be very paying.'

The thin, dark-haired little man was eating his food ravenously, as though he hadn't eaten for a week, but, Michael noticed, that all the while he ate he kept giving them furtive and curious glances.

'What are we going to do next?' asked Ann, after the elderly woman had given them the change and Michael had slipped a coin under his plate.

'Well,' he answered, 'I suggest that we explore the country round here. If we're going to live in the neighbourhood we may as well know something about it. Perhaps, we'll find a nice-looking hotel where we can have dinner and put up for the night.'

Ann readily agreed with the suggestion. They got up and went out to the car. Although it was nearly the end of summer, it was a lovely, warm evening with a clear sky. The sun was flooding the whole length of the High Street, and beyond, where it appeared to straggle away into tree-crested hills and open fields, the view was beautiful.

'I think,' said Ann, when Michael had started the car, 'that I'd like to stay for more than one night, if we can find a nice place. After all, we've got to be back on Monday to see what news Mr. Yardle has about the house.'

'We'll see what we can find,' said Michael. 'We'll go on up this street and see what we come to.'

There was no real end to the High

Street. It frayed away into a winding, hedge-lined road with here and there a small cottage set in a gaily-hued garden to break the line of green. The entrance to a large farm, with a pretty whitewashed house and several haystacks, barns, and cowsheds, lay a mile farther on, and then they found themselves in completely open country. Meadows and fields, stretching away to long lines of woods, bounded the road on either side, unbroken by any sign of habitation.

'Which way does Bracken Cottage lie?' inquired Ann.

'Somewhere behind us,' answered Michael. 'We're going away from it at the moment.'

He happened to glance in the mirror that reflected the road behind. A good way away in their rear, a motorcycle was following them. As he caught sight of it, the sun struck a spark of red from the machine.

It was too far away to be sure, but he thought it was the same motorcycle that had brought the dark-haired man to Peg's Kitchen.

Was he following them?

It might be a coincidence, of course. Even if it were the same motorcycle there were several reasons why the owner might be travelling in the same direction.

But it was queer.

He mentioned it to Ann, and she twisted round in her seat to look through the little window at the back of the car. The distance between it and the following motorcycle had lessened. The white crash helmet of the rider gleamed in the sun. But nearly all motorcyclists wore white crash helmets . . .

The road turned sharply and came out into a broader road that ran at right angles to it. A signpost faced them with two extended arms pointing to the left and to the right. Michael slowed down the car and read;

''Cherriton, two and a half miles, Harvest Green, one mile'. Which shall it be, darling?'

'Harvest Green,' answered Ann promptly. 'It sounds nice.'

'Places never live up to their names,' said Michael, as he turned to the right, 'but we can only hope for the best.'

He looked in the mirror again,

The motorcyclist was moving steadily along behind them.

3

Harvest Green proved to be equal to its name. It was a tiny little village, scarcely more than a hamlet, set on a dip between wooded hillsides and undulating downs. There were a few quaintly shaped cottages clustered round a tiny green, and one small general shop that appeared to sell everything from vegetables to bootlaces.

Just beyond the green, standing back from the road in a paved courtyard, was one of the most attractive inns that Michael had ever seen. It was a long, low, whitewashed building, with a thatched roof. In front of the small, leaded casements were yellow-painted window boxes filled with varicoloured petunias, and this altogether delightful establishment rejoiced in the name of The Wheatsheaf, which Michael thought was most appropriate, considering the name of the place it was in.

'We're in luck,' he said, as he brought the car to a halt in the courtyard. 'I hope that they can manage to fix us up.'

He got out, helped Ann out, and they both went over to the main entrance. Over the door, in black lettering, he read the name of the proprietress, 'Mrs. Amelia Sugden', and rang the bell.

After a few minutes' delay the door was opened by a pleasant-faced little woman with grey hair, a round, shining, red face, and the blackest of black twinkling eyes.

'Good evening,' said Michael. 'Are you Mrs. Sugden?'

'That's right,' answered the little woman, and her black eyes flashed from him to Ann. 'What is it you want?'

Michael explained.

'Come in,' said Mrs. Sugden, 'I think I can manage to put you and your wife up for a few nights. I can't do anything fancy in the way of food, but if you're satisfied with good, plain, wholesome cooking, I can give it you, and plenty of it.'

'We're not in the least faddy about food,' said Ann.

'That's all right then,' said Mrs.

Sugden. 'Come along upstairs and I'll show you the room.'

They followed her up the staircase, along a short corridor, and she opened the door of a room near the end.

'There you are,' she said, ushering them in. 'The bathroom's just opposite.'

It was a low-ceilinged room with white walls and chintz curtains that matched a chintz bedspread on the oaken bed. There was a faint smell of lavender in the atmosphere and the whole place looked scrubbed and scrupulously clean.

'Oh,' said Ann, looking round, 'I like this.'

'There's a parlour downstairs where you can have your meals. Just at the back of the bar. You can use it as a sitting room, if you wish. It'll be quite private.'

Michael settled the terms, which were very moderate, and went out to the car to fetch the luggage.

'I don't know what time you'd like your dinner,' said Mrs. Sugden, as he came back with their suitcases, 'but you can have it when you like. It'll be cold tonight. Roast beef, pickles, potato salad, and a gooseberry pie to follow.'

'It sounds wonderful,' said Michael. 'I think we'll have it about seven, if that suits you.'

'I told you, you can have it when you like,' she answered. 'I'll get you some clean towels and make up the bed while you're at dinner.'

While Ann unpacked their belongings, Michael had a wash and went down to explore.

The bar was quite large with a ceiling of real old oak beams and panelled walls. The bar itself was a semi-circular arrangement in one corner, and there were numerous oak tables and chairs scattered about. There was an archway behind the bar, leading to a passage, and, almost opposite the archway, a door which Michael took to be the door to the parlour which Mrs. Sugden had mentioned. He found his way round to it, opened it, and peeped in.

It was a pleasant room, not overcrowded with furniture like so many of its kind, and its casement windows opened on to a large and colourful garden,

It was, thought Michael, the greatest bit of luck in the world to have found a place like this. It would be quite pleasant to stay here for a few days while they explored the neighbourhood, and waited until it was time to keep their appointment with Mr. Yardle. The thought of Yardle reminded him of the motorcyclist.

Had the man really been following them? If he had, what on earth could be his reason? Just because he had overheard a mention of Bracken Cottage? That seemed ridiculous. The whole thing must have been a coincidence. There had been no sign of the motorcyclist when he had gone out to collect the suitcases. Most likely he was miles away by now. It was just that he had happened to be travelling in the same direction. That was all there was to it . . .

* * *

Michael and Ann spent a pleasant weekend at The Wheatsheaf. The food, although plain, was beautifully cooked, and Mrs. Sugden had made an understatement when she had said there was plenty of it. There was far too much.

They spent the greater part of their time exploring the neighbourhood, discovering many places that pleased them. The name of Bracken Cottage was derived, they found out, from the name, Bracken Bottom, a small village near which it was sited. They went, on the Saturday, for another look at the house and found that they were as pleased with it, on this second visit, as they had been on the first. On the way back to The Wheatsheaf Ann was planning all the decorations she would like.

'You're rather taking things for granted, aren't you, darling?' said Michael, smiling. 'We haven't got the place yet.'

'I'm sure we shall get it,' answered Ann confidently. 'I'd like to do all the painting ourselves, Michael — inside, I mean. What do you feel about it?'

'It would be rather fun,' agreed Michael, who was fond of pottering about doing odd jobs.

'Workmen aren't too good these days,'

said his wife. 'I'm sure we'd make a better job of it ourselves and, at least, we'd get just what we want.'

On the Monday afternoon they set off to keep their appointment with Mr. Yardle. They reached the office in the High Street just before four o'clock and found the clerk reading another book with an even more lurid cover than the other.

'I'm afraid you can't see Mr. Yardle,' he said, in reply to Michael's question. 'He isn't in.'

'When are you expecting him?' asked Michael.

The clerk looked rather confused.

'Well, I can't rightly say, sir,' he answered. 'You see, Mr. Yardle 'asn't been here since Friday mornin'.'

Michael frowned.

'But we had an appointment with him for today,' he said. 'You remember I called here on Wednesday about the house, Bracken Cottage . . . '

'Yes, sir, I remember,' said the clerk. 'I think Mr. Yardle had a letter about it on Friday morning . . . '

Michael thought for a moment.

'We'll go and have some tea and come back,' he said. 'If Mr. Yardle comes in meanwhile, will you tell him we called and will be coming back?'

The clerk promised that he would, and they left. They had tea at Peg's Kitchen again. This time there were two other people there, an old lady and a girl, sitting at the table previously occupied by the motorcyclist. They had seen no more of him, and Michael concluded that it had been nothing more than a coincidence that he had appeared to have been following them.

It was a quarter to five when they returned to the estate agents, but Mr. Yardle had not come back, neither had there been any word from him. They waited until nearly six, when signs of impatience on the part of the clerk warned them that he was waiting to close the office.

Michael, feeling in rather a bad temper, left a note for the estate agent saying that he would call again on the following day and giving The Wheatsheaf as his temporary address.

'He's probably having a long weekend,' said Ann as they went back to the car.

'That's all very well,' grunted Michael, who was thoroughly irritable, 'but when a man makes an appointment, you expect him to keep it.'

'They're not very businesslike in these places,' said Ann. 'I suppose time doesn't matter so much in the country.'

But Mr. Yardle had not returned when they called on the following day.

'I don't understand it, sir,' said the clerk, and he looked genuinely uneasy. 'He's never done such a thing before . . . '

'Have you got in touch with his house?' asked Michael.

The clerk nodded.

'He 'asn't been back there, since he left on Friday mornin',' he said.

'What time did he leave here on Friday?' inquired Michael.

'Round about twelve o'clock,' answered the clerk.

'Was he walking, or did he go by car?'

'He went in 'is car,' said the clerk. 'I

don't quite know what I ought to do, an' that's a fact.'

'Hasn't Mr. Yardle any family — couldn't you get in touch with them?' suggested Michael.

The clerk shook his head.

'He 'asn't got any family,' he said. 'At least I've never heard him mention any. He lived alone in one of the new flats.'

'Well, all I can suggest is that if he doesn't come back by tomorrow you inform the police,' said Michael. 'He may have met with an accident . . . '

'I'd've 'eard, wouldn't I?' said the clerk.

'You might not. Anyhow, that's the best thing you can do.' Michael frowned. 'I suppose you can't find this letter he received from Mrs. Newsome? I'd like to know what she says about the house.'

The clerk appeared a little reluctant to disturb his employers papers, but he eventually agreed to 'have a look'.

Going through into the inner office, he presently reappeared carrying a letter.

'This is it,' he said and handed it to Michael.

The paper was of good quality; the

address printed in neat copperplate at the head of the blue sheet in darker blue lettering. It read:

17 Roseacre Gardens,
Camsford
Thursday.

Cobb & Yardle,
Estate Agents,
High Street,
West Dittersham.

Dear Sir,

In reply to your letter regarding the property, Bracken Cottage, I should be willing to dispose of this if the price offered is a reasonable one. I suggest that you should make an appointment, or call and see me, to discuss the matter further.

Yours faithfully,
Emily Newsome. .

'What does she say?' asked Ann.

'She's willing to sell the house if the price is reasonable,' answered Michael. 'It depends on what she calls reasonable.' He turned to the clerk. 'Do you think that Mr. Yardle could have gone to see Mrs. Newsome on the Friday morning?' he asked. 'This letter suggests that he should call on her.'

The clerk looked dubious.

'He always told me if he was going to keep any appointment,' he said. 'He couldn't 'ave been there all this time, could 'e?'

Michael was forced to admit that it was scarcely likely. The whole thing was a mystery. What could have happened to Yardle? A man didn't suddenly leave his business and disappear unless there was some very sound reason for it. Perhaps there was. Perhaps Yardle's affairs were in a mess. That might be at the bottom of it . . .

Michael decided that, whatever the reason was, it was no business of his. His business was to buy Bracken Cottage if the owner would accept a reasonable offer. The thing to do was to go and see Mrs. Newsome himself. It was, apparently, no good waiting for Yardle to return.

Having come to this conclusion he handed the letter back to the clerk, after noting the address, asked him to let him know at once if there was any news of Mr. Yardle, and he and Ann took their departure.

'What do we do now?' she asked as they got back in the car.

'We'll go and see Mrs. Newsome ourselves,' replied Michael promptly. 'If Yardle comes back he can still handle the matter, but it's no good wasting any more time.'

'It's a very queer thing — his going off like that,' said Ann thoughtfully.

'He may have had a very good reason,' said Michael. 'It looks to me as though he's in some kind of financial difficulties . . . '

'I suppose there isn't any 'Cobb'?' said Ann.

'Obviously not,' replied her husband, skilfully avoiding a large coal lorry that was trying to turn in the narrow street. 'If there was, that young clerk would have got in touch with him.'

They reached Camsford soon after

seven o'clock and inquired the way to Roseacre Gardens. It proved to be a quiet road, lined with nice-looking houses set back behind neat front gardens. Number seventeen was a double-fronted house with bay windows on either side of a yellow painted front door.

They walked up a crazy-paved path between rows of bush and standard roses, and Michael rang the bell. There was a short delay, and then the door was opened by a middle-aged woman in black. She was stout, with short dark hair and rather protruding pale eyes.

'Is it possible to see Mrs. Newsome?' asked Michael.

The woman looked at him rather blankly.

'What's it about?' she demanded in a harsh voice that sounded as though she had a permanently dry throat.

Michael explained.

'I'll go and see,' said the woman. She started to close the door, thought better of it, and went away into a room on the right of the hall, leaving them standing on the step. After a few seconds she came back.

'Will you come in?' she said, and ushered them into the hall.

Ann noticed that the furniture was plain but of good quality. The carpet was thick and soft under her feet, and everything was spotless and polished. There was a faint smell of beeswax and turpentine in the atmosphere, which was not entirely masked by the perfume from a huge bowl of roses that stood on a table against one wall.

Conducting them over to the door on the right, the woman opened it and stood aside for them to enter. The room beyond was the drawing room. It was a large room with a window at either end, and, like the hall, plainly but comfortably furnished.

In a large easy chair at one side of the fireplace sat a thin woman with one of the ugliest faces Michael thought he had ever seen. It was so seamed and lined with wrinkles that it was impossible to judge her age, and on the thin upper lip was the dark shadow of a moustache. From her hands, which were white, smooth, and beautifully shaped, she couldn't have been very old. Possibly somewhere in her early fifties. But if her face was ugly, her voice, in startling contrast, was really beautiful. It was low and melodious with a musical cadence that was a pleasure to listen to.

Michael thought that if you closed your eyes, you would imagine that it was a young girl speaking.

She looked quickly from Ann to Michael and back again.

'Please come and sit down,' she said, indicating a large settee that was set before the fireplace. 'I understand you are the people who wish to buy my house, Bracken Cottage?'

'Yes, if we can agree on the price,' said Michael. He waited for Ann to seat herself and then took his place beside her.

'I want two thousand five hundred,' said Mrs. Newsome promptly. 'Neither more nor less. If that is too much for you there is no need to discuss the matter further.'

'I am quite prepared to agree to that,' said Michael. 'It was the amount I had in mind.'

Mrs. Newsome inclined her head.

'You've seen the house, of course?' she said.

Ann explained how they had found it.

'I was wondering that,' said Mrs. Newsome. 'It has not been advertised for several years so it puzzled me how you knew anything about it. You like it, do you?'

'I think it's charming,' answered Ann. 'I'm dying to move in.'

'Well, it shouldn't be long before you can,' said Mrs. Newsome. 'My solicitors will attend to the matter at once. Do you wish the sale to be done through the agents who wrote to me?'

'I think it would be better if your solicitors got in touch with my own solicitors,' said Michael. 'Mr. Yardle is not available, apparently.'

He related the unaccountable disappearance of the estate agent. Mrs. Newsome listened with interest.

'Got himself in some sort of trouble, I should think,' she remarked. 'I suppose you know that the house originally belonged to my brother, William Crayle, who was hanged for murder?'

Michael nodded.

'If you hadn't known about that, you soon would,' said Mrs. Newsome. 'The people at Bracken Bottom would have been only too eager to tell you. The place has a very bad reputation. That's why I've never sold it. I had several offers but the price offered was ridiculous.'

Behind her downrightness in telling them about her brother, Michael thought he detected a touch of bitterness and defiance. She had succeeded in living down the notoriety and the scandal, but the memory still hurt and rankled.

'I'm surprised,' she said, turning to Ann, 'that a young girl like you should wish to live at Bracken Cottage. Won't you find it very lonely?'

'I love the country,' said Ann, 'and we have a flat in London we can pop up to whenever we want a change of scene. Bracken Cottage will be ideal for Michael. He'll be able to write without any distractions.'

'Your husband is an author, is he?' said Mrs. Newsome. 'I don't read very much myself. My hobbies are gardening and cooking. I flatter myself that I am an expert at both.'

The stout woman who had let them in, entered with a tray on which were three glasses of sherry.

'I always have a glass of sherry before dinner,' said Mrs. Newsome. 'I hope you will join me? If you like sherry you will find this quite a good one,'

It was an excellent sherry. Michael decided that Mrs. Newsome looked after herself extremely well. He supposed that her husband had left her well provided for — or had she inherited more from her brother than Bracken Cottage?

When they had finished the sherry they took their leave. Mrs. Newsome promised to notify her solicitors at once and ask them to do everything possible to facilitate the completion of the sale.

As they left the house and crossed the pavement to the car, a motorcyclist roared past. Michael thought he recognized the red machine that had followed them to Harvest Green. But it was moving so quickly he couldn't be sure.

4

Michael paid the full amount of the purchase price to his solicitors and, at their request, received from Mrs. Newsome's solicitors permission to take possession of Bracken Cottage immediately. There was a certain amount of legal business still to be transacted before they received the title deeds, but neither Ann nor Michael were particularly interested in these formalities. All they wished to do was to get down to the cottage and start work on the new decorations.

There was no further news of Yardle. He had completely disappeared and, although the matter was in the hands of the police, no explanation for his strange disappearance had come to light. The police were, as a matter of fact, in rather a delicate position. The man had done nothing criminal and, although there were a certain number of small bills owing, there was a considerable sum to his credit at the bank. If a person chooses to vanish, apparently of his own free will, and performs no criminal act by doing so, the authorities are rather handicapped.

It was a strange thing to have happened, all the same, and Michael wondered just what lay at the bottom of it. The office in West Dittersham High Street had been closed. Presumably the youthful clerk had found another job, and the matter of Mr. Yardle's disappearance became almost forgotten.

The leaves of the trees had turned russet by the time Ann and Michael had completed their work on the interior of their new home, and the furniture that they had bought had been set in its place. The only thing that they had not done themselves had been the kitchen. This had required so much alteration that Ann had arranged with a firm in Camsford, who specialized in the work, to come and do it.

During the period of getting the place ready for habitation, they had continued to stay at The Wheatsheaf. Mrs. Sugden looked after them like a mother and was genuinely interested in hearing all about the improvements Ann was making at the cottage.

There was one thing that rather worried Ann. The apparently complete impossibility of getting anyone to come to do the cleaning.

She had got hold of the name and address of a woman — a Mrs. Candy — who lived at Bracken Bottom, and late one afternoon, the day after they had moved into their new home permanently, she decided to call on the woman and try and arrange for her to come daily and do such cleaning as was necessary.

Mrs. Candy lived in a small cottage on the outskirts of the village, her husband worked on a nearby farm, and it was getting dusk when Michael brought the car to a halt opposite the house.

'This is the place,' he said. 'I'll come in with you. It will add dignity and tone to the interview.' '

'Idiot!' said Ann. 'You'd better let me do the talking.'

Mrs. Candy was a small, stringy woman, with untidy brown hair and a sharp and rather shrewish expression. She eyed them without any visible signs of friendliness.

'What would you be wantin'?' she demanded curtly.

'I'm Mrs. Wayland,' said Ann pleasantly. 'My husband and I have just moved into Bracken Cottage. I understand that you — '

'You're livin' in the 'ouse now?' interrupted the woman sharply.

'We moved in yesterday,' said Ann. 'I'm looking for somebody to come in daily to do the cleaning . . . '

The woman shook her head. 'Not me, Mum,' she said.

'You are Mrs. Candy, aren't you?' asked Ann.

'Yes, that's me,' answered the woman.

'Well, I was told that you did go out cleaning — '

'Not at Bracken Cottage I don't,' declared Mrs. Candy, shaking her head again. 'I wouldn't come nigh the place for all the tea in China.'

'Why not?' demanded Michael.

'An' you won't get nobody in these

parts to come, neither,' said Mrs. Candy emphatically. 'Not if yer was to offer 'em a 'undred pound.'

'But why?' asked Ann in astonishment. 'What's the matter with the place?'

'You'll find out before you've bin there long,' answered Mrs. Candy. 'There's queer things goes on at Ghost 'Ouse . . . '

'Ghost House?' repeated Ann.

'That's what they call it round 'ere,' said the woman. 'Belonged to Crayle, the murderer, it did — '

'But, surely,' broke in Michael, 'that doesn't affect the house? Crayle's dead . . . '

'There's some what believe that those what die a violent death don't rest easy in their graves,' said Mrs. Candy. 'Hung, 'e was,' she added with relish.

'But that's ridiculous,' said Ann.

'Is it, Mum?' said Mrs. Candy. 'Well, it's your business, not mine. If you take my advice, you'll clear out o' that place jest as quick as you can. I wouldn't live there, no, not if it was give me rent free . . . '

'You must have some reason for feeling

like that, Mrs. Candy,' said Michael. 'A better reason than just because the house once belonged to a murderer . . . '

'Maybe I have an' maybe I 'aven't,' said the woman. 'The place is evil an' best left alone, in my opinion. The woods are too close an' too thick. They 'ide things that creep out in the night . . . '

Michael laughed and she gave a sharp, angry glance.

'You can laugh,' she said, 'but it's still daylight an' you ain't bin there long. Maybe you'll not be laughing soon. Things 'appen to people in Bracken Bottom . . . '

'What kind of things?' asked Ann.

The woman shook her head darkly.

'All kinds of things,' she said. 'There's a short cut through them woods, from 'ere to Bracken Cottage. People used ter use it. They don't no more — not after what 'appened to young 'Arry.'

'What happened to young Harry?' demanded Michael.

Again Mrs. Candy shook her head.

'Nobody rightly knows what 'e see,' she said. 'There weren't nuthin' the matter with 'im afore, but 'e 'ad ter be taken to the asylum after. 'E see somethin' but what it were nobody knows.'

Michael tried to argue with her, but it was of no avail.

She refused to listen. It was her belief that there was something in and around Bracken Cottage that was evil and dangerous, and nothing either Michael or Ann could say would alter this belief,

'I'm sorry you should've 'ad all yer trouble comin' 'ere fer nuthin',' she said finally. 'I'd come an' work fer you, if it was anywhere else, but not there. An' yer won't get no one to, I can promise you that. If yer take my tip, you'll see that yer doors is bolted an' yer winders fastened after dark, an' you won't go outside.'

'Well,' said Ann as they returned to the car, 'would you believe anybody could be so stupid?'

'They get fixed ideas about things in the country,' answered Michael, gently letting in the clutch and sending the car slowly down the road. 'The whole thing's pure superstition, of course. Crayle was a murderer and he was hanged, therefore the cottage he owned and lived in must be evil, too.'

'Do you think young 'Arry really saw anything?' asked Ann.

'Something scared the wits out of him obviously,' said Michael. 'But I don't expect he was very bright to begin with. It could have been sheer imagination — the sight of a bush or a tree in the dark . . . '

'It's very annoying,' she said, frowning. 'And it's going to be very awkward. I must get somebody to do the cleaning, darling. I can't manage it all on my own.'

'You won't get anyone from here,' said Michael. 'The only thing I can suggest is that we try and find somebody to live in. We've got an extra room.'

'That's going to be almost as difficult,' she said. 'You just can't get servants these days, particularly in the country. They want somewhere where there are cinemas and dances . . . '

'We can but try,' answered Michael. 'I'll ring up the nearest employment agency tomorrow.'

Ann was silent for a minute or two and then she said:

'What do you think she meant by 'the things that creep out of the woods at night'?'

Michael laughed.

'I don't suppose she knows,' he said. 'Don't you start getting ideas, darling, just because a silly woman like Mrs. Candy talks a lot of poppycock . . . '

'Something must have started the poppycock, Michael,' she said.

'Something did,' he answered. 'Crayle. There's nothing wrong with the house. It's charming.'

They were running down the road that led to the gate that gave admittance to the drive to Bracken Cottage. Michael switched on the headlights because, by now, it was getting dark. Just as he brought the car to a stop, preparatory to getting out and opening the gate, he thought he caught sight of something moving among the bushes of the short drive. It might have been a trick of the imagination, but it looked as though a shadow had flitted from one bush to another. He said nothing to Ann, but when he had seen her safely inside the house, he made an excuse about fetching his cigarettes from the car to go out again. Coming back to the place where he thought he had seen the moving shadow, he made a thorough search. But he found nothing. The soft ground under the bushes showed several footprints but they could easily have been his own, or the workmen who had reconstructed the kitchen.

In the cosy warmth of the well-lighted and comfortably furnished sitting room, after a pleasant meal, he almost forgot about the matter. And then something reminded him.

Ann was pottering about rearranging oddments, vases, ornaments, trying them in various different places for a better effect. She had just carried a lamp from a table to the top of the long, low bookcase that occupied the whole of one wall, when he put his question:

'When did you oil the gate, darling?'

She looked round in surprise.

'Oil the gate?' she repeated. 'I haven't oiled the gate, if you mean the main gate that squeaks so badly.'

But that was just it. That was what he had suddenly remembered.

The gate hadn't squeaked!

It had opened without a sound!

He hadn't noticed it at the time because of his preoccupation with the moving shadow in the bushes. But it hadn't squeaked!

Somebody had oiled it. Who and why?

One of the things that crept out of the woods at night?

'Why did you ask me that?' said Ann, still standing with the lamp in her hand.

'I just wondered,' answered Michael evasively. 'I've always been going to do it, but I've never got around to it . . . '

She set the lamp down carefully on the top of the bookcase and came over to the fire.

'The gate didn't creak when you opened it tonight,' she said. 'I remember now. But it creaked when we went out, to go to Mrs. Candy's.'

Michael had remembered that too.

She looked at him seriously.

'Who oiled it, Michael?' she said.

He shook his head.

‘I don’t know,’ he replied.

Ann helped herself to a cigarette from the box on the low table in front of the settee.

‘Somebody must have done it while we were out,’ she said.

‘Who?’ asked Michael. ‘Why on earth should anyone want to oil our gate?’

He got up and lighted her cigarette for her.

‘Because,’ said Ann gravely, ‘it creaked. It creaked so loudly that we could hear it inside the house. It was as good as a bell. Nobody could come through that gate without us knowing, Michael.’

‘Are you suggesting that somebody wants to come through without letting us know?’ inquired Michael.

‘Can you suggest any other reason why somebody should take the trouble to oil our gate?’ she retorted.

‘No,’ said Michael, ‘I can’t . . . But it’s absurd. Why should anyone want to come here without us knowing?’

She blew out a thin stream of smoke from her pursed lips.

‘I’m beginning to think there was

something in what that woman said,' she answered.

'Nonsense,' he said. 'There must be a simple explanation, darling . . . '

'All right, you give me one,' she said.

But he couldn't.

'I'm going to take Mrs. Candy's advice and bolt all the doors and fasten the windows at night in future,' said Ann firmly.

'What on earth do you expect?' he asked lightly. 'Burglars?'

'There's no harm in taking precautions,' she replied. 'I don't like that oiled gate, Michael.'

Michael didn't like it, either, but he didn't say so.

The oiled gate was only the first in a series of queer things that happened in the days to come, and culminated eventually in such a horrible climax . . .

The second of these occurred two days later.

Ann and Michael had been over to the nearest town — Havershot — to do some shopping. On their return they discovered a man in the garden armed with a large sheet of paper pinned to a board, and a steel measuring tape, with which he was, apparently, engaged in measuring the outside of the cottage.

He was an unprepossessing individual, rather shabbily dressed in a dirty raincoat, with shoes that were very down at heel and badly needed cleaning. On his chin was a two-days' growth of stubbly beard, and his long, thin nose was crooked. He seemed to be startled at their appearance.

But he had a ready explanation when Michael demanded to know who he was and what he was doing there.

He was making a survey for the council, he said. There was a new map of the district being prepared.

Michael happened to get a glance at the paper on his board. It contained a crude plan of Bracken Cottage, certainly not the kind of plan that a surveyor would make.

After he'd gone, Michael took the trouble to go to the nearest telephone, and telephone to the council offices for the district. It took him some time to get on to the right department, but he succeeded at last. There was no new map of the district contemplated and they knew nothing whatever about any survey.

The man with the steel tape measure had lied.

Whatever the reason was which had brought him to Bracken Cottage, it was not on behalf of the council.

The third strange thing that took place was a little more alarming. They came down one morning to find an envelope on the mat. The post did not reach them until midday, but this had not come through the post. It had been delivered by hand.

It was addressed to 'Mr. Michael Wayland' and he opened it.

Inside he found a half sheet of cheap paper, torn, from the look of it, out of an exercise book. On it, in capital letters, printed in pencil, was the following:

'UNLESS YOU WANT TROUBLE
YOU'D BETTER CLEAR OUT'

Michael took the note to the local police, but they seemed to treat it as a practical joke more than anything to be taken seriously. Nor were they very impressed when he told them about the oiled gate and the man with the measuring tape. But they promised to look into the matter, which Michael judged to be tantamount to doing nothing at all.

The fourth incident was completely inexplicable.

Mrs. Candy had mentioned, during their brief interview with her, that there was a short cut through the woods to Bracken Bottom. Running out of cigarettes one morning, and feeling that he'd like a walk, Michael decided to take this short cut, if he could find it, and buy some cigarettes at the little general shop in the village.

He found the short cut, which wound through the woods near the back of the cottage. It was a pleasant walk, the little path twisting and turning in and out among the trees. The undergrowth was thick farther in the depth of the wood, and on his way back, after getting his cigarettes, he noticed something glint in the middle of a particularly dense patch. Wondering what it was, he went over to have a closer look.

Almost entirely concealed in the undergrowth, except for the portion of handlebar, which had first attracted his attention, was a motorcycle. It had evidently been there for some time because there were patches of fresh rust where the plating had worn off, but there was no mistaking the bright red paint of the frame.

It was the motorcycle belonging to the thin, dark-haired little man who had followed them from the teashop in West Dittersham High Street.

5

Michael stared down at his find in complete bewilderment. What on earth was it doing there? Only a complete lunatic would leave an expensive motorcycle to rust under a mass of undergrowth. Perhaps the owner was somewhere in the neighbourhood? Had he hidden the machine there while he went somewhere on foot? But the bike looked as if it had been there for several days. He'd hardly be likely to leave it there for so long. Anybody might have come along and found it.

Michael frowned, still staring at the machine It struck him that he might discover some clue to its owner in the tool-bag. With some little difficulty, for it had been pushed well into the thicket of undergrowth, Michael succeeded in pulling it out from its hiding place sufficiently to get at the tool-bag. But it contained tools and nothing more. There was a mica-covered pocket in the leather in which to slip the name and address of the owner but it was empty.

He took out his wallet, however, and noted down the number — 0X371. That might come in useful. The identity of the dark-haired man could be traced through that, if it was necessary.

The question was, what ought he to do about the motorcycle? Certainly it was no affair of his. Should he just leave it where he had found it, or ought he to notify the police?

His previous experience with the local police had not been a particularly happy one, and he decided, after a little thought, to leave the motorcycle where it was.

He thrust it back in the covering undergrowth, carefully arranging it so that not even the smallest portion was visible to give its presence away to anyone who might pass that way.

He was very thoughtful as he walked slowly back to Bracken Cottage. There was something very puzzling going on. The little dark man had obviously been startled when he had heard Ann mention the name of the house in the teashop that afternoon, and apparently he had followed them. This might be a coincidence, but in view of the discovery of the motorcycle, Michael was inclined to think that it was nothing of the sort. Then there was the queer incident of the complete and unexplained disappearance of the estate agent, Yardle, the almost equally queer incidents of the oiled gate, the man with the tape measure, the note through the door, with its inexplicable warning, and now his discovery of the discarded motorcycle.

Bracken Cottage seemed to have become the focal point for a series of irritating and unexplainable happenings, and Michael wondered what was at the bottom of it all.

Unless the note was a hoax, which was obviously the opinion of the police, somebody wanted them out of the house. It was all very strange and disturbing, and the strangest and most disturbing of all was his recent discovery.

What had happened to the owner of

the motorcycle? Why had he gone off and left the machine where Michael had found it?

It might have nothing to do with the other incidents at all, but Michael was of the opinion that they all fitted together somehow. He felt a vague sense of uneasiness. Since they had come to Bracken Bottom they seemed to have been caught up in some unaccountable mystery, all the more worrying because it was unaccountable.

Michael decided to say nothing to Ann about the motorcycle. He had no wish to alarm her any more than was necessary, but he made up his mind to find out all he could about William Crayle, and the details of the murder for which he had been hanged. Hoppy was the man who could help him there, and as soon as he got back to the cottage, he went up to his study and wrote a letter to Hoppy, asking him if he could find the time to come down and see them.

He posted this immediately after lunch and felt better.

Ann was still having to cope with all the work. The agency had promised to do their best to find someone to live in, but, up to now, they had been unsuccessful. Michael had put an advertisement in the local paper without any better result. Failing everything else, they decided, he would have to run up to London and try one of the agencies there.

That evening there was a further incident in the series.

They had finished dinner, and Ann was in the kitchen washing up the dishes. Michael heard her scream, and the smash of china, and ran out of the sitting room in alarm to see what had happened.

Ann was staring at the kitchen window, the scattered remains of a plate at her feet. Her face was the colour of chalk.

'What's the matter, darling?' demanded Michael anxiously. 'Did you hurt yourself?'

She gulped.

'No . . . I saw something . . . somebody . . . outside the window,' she gasped with difficulty.

'Are you sure?' asked Michael.

'Yes . . . I saw them move . . . '

Michael ran to the back door and opened it.

'Where are you going?' cried Ann, catching him by the arm. 'Don't go out there . . . '

'Nonsense,' said Michael, freeing himself. 'If there is somebody lurking about the place, I'm going to find them.'

'Be careful,' she called after him. 'Do be careful, Michael.'

He made a thorough search of the garden as best he could in the darkness, but he found nobody. Everything was quite silent. He came back a little breathless.

'There's nobody there,' he panted, shutting the back door and turning the key in the lock.

'There was,' said Ann emphatically. 'It was a man, I think. I saw his face in the light from the window . . . '

'Well, he must have cleared off pretty quickly,' said Michael. 'What was he like?'

She shook her head.

'I don't know . . . I only caught a glimpse of him. I couldn't be sure that it was a man . . . '

She stooped and began to pick up the pieces of the broken plate.

'I'll finish washing the dishes,' said Michael. 'You come in to the sitting room and have a drink. You look as white as a ghost.'

'It did startle me,' she said, as she followed him into the sitting room. 'It was silly . . . '

Michael went over to the drinks table and poured her out a stiff tot of Johnnie Walker.

'Drink that — neat,' he ordered. 'It'll pull you together.'

She obeyed.

'Now, have a cigarette,' said Michael. He gave her one and lit it. 'You're quite sure you did see something?' he asked after a pause. 'It wasn't some kind of reflection in the window glass?'

'No,' answered Ann positively. 'There was somebody. I think they were on the point of looking in the window when I saw them.'

'There wasn't a sound or a movement when I went out,' declared Michael. 'I think I'll have a spot of

Johnnie Walker myself.'

She inhaled the smoke of her cigarette deeply and let it trickle slowly from her nostrils. He saw, as he poured himself out the whisky, that her hand was trembling slightly.

'Michael,' she said, 'what's the meaning of it all? What's happening round here? I'm getting frightened . . . '

'There's nothing to be frightened of, darling,' he said reassuringly, though he wasn't feeling any too certain himself.

'I am frightened,' she said. 'It's no use pretending — I am . . . '

Michael had to admit that he was more than a little uneasy himself. But he kept his uneasiness to himself.

* * *

For the following two days, life at Bracken Cottage was devoid of any unusual incident. Events were working to a climax, but neither Ann nor Michael had any prevision of this and so they carried on their normal lives, although they both wondered what the past series of incidents meant and devoutly hoped that there would be no more.

In answer to Michael's letter to Bob Hopkins there arrived on the third day a wire from that energetic individual. It was brief and to the point:

'MEET ME HAVERSHOT SATION THREE O'CLOCK FRIDAY. HOPPY'

The wire had been sent from Fleet Street on the previous night. Today was Friday and, after lunch, Michael and Ann set off for Havershot. They were glad that Hoppy was coming down for the little, red-haired reporter was an equally good friend of both of them.

The London train steamed into Havershot station five minutes late, and among the first passengers to alight they caught sight of the thin, wiry figure of Hoppy. He was wearing an old, soiled raincoat — his habitual attire in the winter — and his flaming hair was as conspicuous as a neon sign, in a country road.

He greeted them with an enormous grin on his freckled face.

'Hello, folks,' he said. 'So you've settled in the wilds, eh? How do you like it?'

'It's a charming house,' said Ann.

There was something in her tone, however, that made the astute Hoppy look at her quickly.

'What's wrong?' he demanded.

Michael laughed.

'You're too sharp, Hoppy,' he said.

'I shouldn't last long on the Messenger, if I wasn't,' retorted Hoppy. 'So there is something wrong?'

'Not wrong exactly,' answered Michael. 'Just queer.'

Hoppy's eyes sparkled.

'Queer, eh?' he said. 'That's good. Maybe there's a story.'

'Maybe there is,' agreed Michael. 'Do you know who Bracken Cottage belonged to originally?'

Hoppy shook his head.

'William Crayle,' said Michael.

'The man who was hanged for shooting Tim Helman,' exclaimed Hoppy. 'And there have been some queer things happening, eh?'

'I'll tell you all about it when we get

home,' said Michael. 'How long can you stay?'

'Until Monday,' replied Hoppy. 'I've got a long weekend off.'

He was only carrying a briefcase, which, he said, contained a suit of pyjamas, a razor, and a toothbrush — all he needed. They escorted him to the waiting car and set off back to Bracken Cottage.

After tea, Michael told Hoppy all that happened, omitting, however, to mention his discovery of the abandoned motor-cycle, which, he decided, to reserve until later when Ann was not present.

Hoppy listened with great interest.

'It's certainly queer enough,' he commented. 'I think there's a story in this, Michael, if we can find out what it's all about.'

'Do you remember the details of the Helman murder?' asked Michael. 'I remember something about it, but only vaguely. What happened exactly?'

Hoppy took out a packet of Woodbines — they were the only cigarettes he ever smoked — lighted one and blew out a cloud of smoke.

'It was an unusual murder,' he said, 'at least for this country. Almost like a gang killing, only there was no gang. Just Helman and Crayle. The whole thing has always been a bit of a mystery. Helman was a crook, one of the men who were concerned with the mailbag robbery six years ago. So far as ever came out, he and Crayle were complete strangers. One night Helman was walking along a country road, just outside Basingstoke, when a car drew in to the side of the road, and he was shot dead. The driver of the car was Crayle. The shooting was, apparently, quite cold-blooded and deliberate, and Crayle would undoubtedly have got away with it, only he was unlucky. A police car was out that night looking for a man who had been molesting women in the district, and Crayle ran bang into it. It was a fair cop, and although he tried to throw the weapon away, it was recovered, and, of course, the bullet out of Helman's body was later proved to have been fired from it. There was no hope for Crayle from the start — '

'But there must have been a motive,' interrupted Michael.

Hoppy shrugged his shoulders.

'If there was, it never came out,' he said. 'The police could find no connection between Helman and Crayle of any sort. So far as was known, they didn't even know each other. They tried to discover what Helman was doing on the country road where he was killed, but that, too, was a mystery. He had taken a train to Basingstoke and walked from the station. What he was doing there, or where he was going when Crayle drove up and shot him, remains unknown to this day.'

'Perhaps he had an appointment to meet Crayle there,' said Michael.

'That was the police theory,' agreed Hoppy. 'But what for?'

'Wouldn't Crayle tell them?' asked Ann.

'Crayle refused to say anything,' answered the reporter. 'He refused to make a statement when he was arrested and he kept his mouth shut all through the trial.'

'What kind of man was he?' asked Michael curiously. 'I mean what was his business?'

'He hadn't any business and, apparently, very little money,' replied Hoppy. 'There was only a hundred or so in his bank account. If ever there was a mystery man, in the true sense of the word, it was Crayle.'

'Well,' remarked Ann with a grimace, 'he seems to have left a legacy of mystery behind him.'

Hoppy nodded and stubbed out his cigarette in the ashtray.

'I'm rather interested in that,' he said thoughtfully. 'I'll get on to my paper in the morning . . . '

'Now, look here, Hoppy,' said Michael. 'We don't want a lot of publicity about this . . . '

'You can trust me,' said Hoppy. 'I won't publish anything — not yet, anyhow. But I smell a big story behind this business of yours, and I want to nose it out. Maybe, they'll let me stay longer than Monday, if you can put me up.'

'You're welcome to stay as long as you

like,' said Michael, heartily, which Ann quickly endorsed.

Later that evening, while she was out in the kitchen, Michael told Hoppy of his discovery of the motorcycle. The reporter was more than interested.

'That's the strangest thing of the lot,' he declared. 'I don't like the look of it, Michael.'

'What do you mean?' asked Michael.

'Do you think this man, whoever he is, would leave his bike lying about like that, if he could help it? It looks to me as though something had happened to him — something pretty serious.'

Michael made a gesture of despair.

'It seems to me as though Ann and I have landed in the middle of a shilling shocker,' he said.

Hoppy looked at him queerly.

'It wouldn't surprise me if you were nearly right,' he said.

6

The *Daily Messenger*, apparently, shared Hoppy's interest in the happenings at Bracken Cottage, for the reporter came back on the following morning, after he had telephoned that enterprising paper's news editor, with the information that he could stay until further notice.

'I've asked 'em to have that number looked up,' he told Michael, when the latter and he were alone. 'Then we shall at least know who your mysterious follower is.'

'We're not certain he was following us,' said Michael.

'Well, in any case, it won't do any harm to know all about him,' said Hoppy. 'This is a mighty intriguing business, in my opinion. I want to know just what's at the bottom of it.'

'So do I,' agreed Michael, 'though not for the same reason. Ann and I bought this place for a little peace and quiet. All this mysterious nonsense is frightening her . . . '

'It might be with reason,' said Hoppy seriously.

'You're hardly comforting,' retorted Michael. 'What the deuce do you imagine is likely to happen?'

'I don't know,' admitted Hoppy.

What *did* happen was something that neither Michael nor Ann expected. It happened just before lunch, and in the most prosaic manner, with an overflow from the main water storage tank. The escape pipe started to pour down into the garden, and since it was so situated that it poured directly on the back door step, deluging anybody who came in or out that way, something had to be done about it.

'The ball-cock's gone wonky,' said Hoppy. 'It's a habit with ball-cocks. Where's the tank?'

Ann explained that it was up in the loft.

'I'll go and see what I can do,' said Hoppy helpfully. 'I'm smaller than Michael, I can get through the trap. I suppose there is a trap? There usually is.'

Michael assured him that there was a trap. It was rather difficult of access because there was no ladder attached. It was necessary to carry up the steps to the top landing.

This they proceeded to do. Michael held the steps while Hoppy climbed up and pushed back the trap. Gripping the sides of the small, square aperture, Hoppy hauled himself up until he was sitting on the edge with his legs dangling in space.

'It's pretty dark up here,' he said. 'Have you got a candle or something?'

'I've a torch,' said Michael. 'I'll go and get it.'

He hurried away down the stairs, found the torch in the kitchen and hurried back.

'Here you are,' he said, handing the torch up to Hoppy.

'Thanks,' said the reporter, and hoisted himself up into the loft.

Michael saw the light from the torch as Hoppy switched it on, and then he heard a sudden sharp exclamation.

'What's the matter?' he called. 'Stubbed your toe?'

There was no answer for a moment, and then Hoppy's voice, strangely altered by the hollow echo of the loft, said in an urgent whisper:

'You'd better come up here, Michael.'

Gingerly, Michael mounted the steps and thrust his head through the aperture of the trap.

'What's the matter?' he asked again.

For answer Hoppy put down his hand and gripped one of Michael's.

'Can you manage, if I pull you?' he asked.

'Yes, I think so,' said Michael. With Hoppy's aid he scrambled up into the loft. 'Now, what's all the excitement about?' he demanded.

'Excitement's right,' grunted Hoppy. 'Take a look at this.'

He directed the light of the torch on a dark something that was huddled up against one of the sloping walls.

'Good grief!' muttered Michael in horrified surprise.

It was the body of a man!

The face was almost covered with a mask of dried blood, but Michael recognized the leather jacket. It was the owner of the motorcycle!

'How on earth did he get here?' he whispered, when he had told the reporter who the man was.

'Not on his own,' answered Hoppy grimly. 'He must have been put here after he was dead.' He went over and, shining his light on the head, he continued: 'Somebody hit him pretty hard. The back of his head is crushed like an eggshell.'

Michael stared down at the body. The dark hair was matted with blood and the leather jacket was streaked and stained.

'When did you last come up here?' asked Hoppy.

'Several weeks ago,' answered Michael, 'but the workmen who were doing the kitchen came up here to do something about the water supply . . . '

He was still staring at the huddled body in a daze of disbelief.

'How long ago was that?' asked the reporter.

'A few days before we moved in,' replied Michael mechanically. 'Nobody's been up here since . . . '

'Somebody has,' said Hoppy. 'Somebody brought this thing up here, and it must've been after the workmen had left and before you arrived. He's been dead for quite a while.'

'What are we going to do?' muttered Michael.

'We'll have to inform the police,' said Hoppy. 'There's no possibility of keeping this thing dark. It's murder. He couldn't have given himself a wound like that.'

'He might have had an accident,' said Michael, and realized what a stupid suggestion it was as soon as he had spoken.

'And come up here on his own?' demanded Hoppy. 'Don't be absurd, Michael. It took a strong man, maybe more than one, to get him up here . . . '

'Perhaps he was killed here,' suggested Michael, but the reporter shook his head.

'I don't think so,' he said. 'There's no trace of blood about, except on the body itself. There would bound to be spatters if the blow had been delivered up here.'

Ann's voice reached them, calling from downstairs.

'The pipe's still overflowing,' she said. 'Can't you do anything?'

'We'll be down in a minute, darling,' called Michael. 'We're just trying to find out what's the matter.' He looked at Hoppy and his expression was worried. 'We shall have to tell her,' he whispered.

'I'm afraid there's no help for it,' said Hoppy. He moved over to the water tank, hoisted himself up on a beam that supported the sloping roof, and peered inside.

'It looks to me,' he said, 'as if the ball has sprung a leak. The best thing we can do is to tie it up so that no more water can enter the tank.' He flashed the light about the loft. 'There's nothing up here I can do it with. Can you get a piece of rope or wire?'

Michael nodded. He lowered himself through the open trap and descended the steps. There was a ball of thick string in his study and in a few seconds he was back with it.

Hoppy tied up the ball cock.

'That's that,' he said. 'That'll stop the overflow, temporarily at any rate. Now we'd better go and tell Ann about — that.' He jerked his head towards the body. 'We'll shut up the trap again. Everything should be left as it is until the police have seen it.'

They came down from the loft and pulled the trap into place. Then they went slowly down the stairs to the kitchen.

'Have you mended it?' asked Ann cheerfully, and then, as she caught sight of their faces: 'What's the matter?'

'I could do with a drink,' said Hoppy. 'Let's go into the sitting room.'

He led the way and Michael and Ann followed.

'What is the matter?' said Ann again. 'You both look as if you'd seen a ghost . . . '

Michael poured out three stiff whiskies, gave one to Ann and one to Hoppy, and then he told her.

Under the make-up, her face whitened. She stared at him with wide, frightened eyes.

'A dead man . . . in the loft?' she said in a voice that went suddenly husky. 'Oh, no . . . '

'I'm afraid it's true,' said Hoppy, gulping his drink, and setting down the empty glass

'Who . . . who is it?' she asked.

'The man on the motorcycle who we thought was following us from the teashop,' answered Michael.

She took a sip of her whisky.

'But why . . . what was he doing here? Why should anyone want to kill him?'

Michael made a gesture of bewilderment.

'Heaven knows,' he exclaimed. 'I suppose it's all mixed up with the other things — the man with the tape measure, that note, and all the rest of it . . . '

'There's not much doubt of that,' said Hoppy.

'And . . . and that's been up there all the time,' muttered Ann, and gave a little shiver. 'I'm glad I didn't know . . . '

'Not a very pleasant thought, is it?' said Michael. 'Never mind, we'll pack up and go to The Wheatsheaf or back to the flat.'

To his surprise Ann shook her head.

'We'll do nothing of the kind,' she said determinedly. 'I like this house and I'm going to stay in it.'

Hoppy patted her shoulder approvingly.

'That's the spirit,' he said. 'We'll see it through. I'm afraid there's going to be a lot of unpleasantness for you both. This can't be kept out of the papers, and that'll mean publicity, but since it's got to happen in any case, I may as well be the first with the news.'

'I suppose there's no avoiding the publicity,' grunted Michael, frowning.

'Not a hope,' said the reporter. 'Once the police are called in — '

'The police?' repeated Ann.

'They'll have to be informed,' said Hoppy. 'Don't worry. I'll be here to help you. I'm bound to be assigned to cover this by the Messenger, and I suppose you'd rather I stayed here than put up at an hotel?'

'Of course,' said Michael.

'I'll go and phone the news editor,' said Hoppy, 'and then we'll get in touch with the police . . . '

* * *

Chief Inspector Bartram of the Havershot C.I.D. was a thickset, grey-haired man with mild brown eyes and a rather large moustache that dropped over a tight-set mouth. He listened to what they had to tell him without interruption, and then he proceeded to fire a battery of questions.

Michael had to go through everything that had happened from the time he and Ann had first seen the house to the time when the body had been discovered. Everything he said was noted down in detail by Sergeant Bishop, also of the Havershot C.I.D., a stout, red-faced, genial-looking man, who looked more like a publican than a detective.

When Bartram had gathered all the information that he could, he became suddenly galvanized into action. A police car was summoned, photographers, fingerprint men, and the police surgeon, were peremptorily sent for, and Chief Inspector Bartram, accompanied by this retinue, set off for Bracken Cottage.

Michael, Ann, and Hoppy followed in the former's car.

They all arrived at the house together,

and under Bartram's orders, the laborious routine involved in an investigation of murder began.

The doctor made his examination of the body. The man had died as the result of a heavy blow on the back of the head, a blow delivered with such force that the bones of the skull had been severely fractured. Death must have been instantaneous. The man had been dead for a considerable time. The doctor was not prepared to state exactly how long, but certainly for several days,

After the doctor had finished, the photographers and fingerprint men took over. The body of the little, dark-haired man was photographed from several angles, and the whole of the loft was carefully gone over for possible prints, particularly the trap giving admittance to it.

By the time this had all been attended to, the ambulance had arrived, and Bartram gave orders for the body to be removed to the mortuary for the post-mortem.

'Now, sir,' said the chief inspector. 'I'd

like to see this motorcycle.'

Michael, accompanied by Hoppy, took him to the place in the wood where he had found the machine hidden.

Bartram, with the assistance of Sergeant Bishop, pulled it out from the concealing undergrowth, and carefully examined it. It yielded nothing of importance, except the number.

'It shouldn't be difficult to establish the identity of the dead man with this,' remarked Bartram. 'Supposing, of course, that the machine belonged to him. It might have been borrowed or pinched. In any case, we'll be able to trace the owner.'

He gave orders for the motorcycle to be removed to Havershot, and he returned to Bracken Cottage with Hoppy and Michael. A constable, who had been brought over with the rest of the retinue, was on guard on the door.

Ann, who had been persuaded, very reluctantly, to stay behind when they went to find the motorcycle, had made coffee, and Bartram and the sergeant accepted a cup gratefully.

'Well,' said the chief inspector, 'it's a

mysterious affair. There doesn't seem to be much doubt that this man was killed somewhere outside the house, and brought in after the workmen had left and before you and your wife took up residence, sir. Though why the murderer should have gone to the trouble an' risk of doing that beats me.'

'Do you think,' said Ann, 'that these other things have anything to do with it?'

Bartram shook his head.

'It's difficult to give any opinion yet, ma'm,' he said.

'The police wouldn't take the note we got, and the strange man with the measuring tape, very seriously, when I reported them,' remarked Michael.

The chief inspector smiled.

'They didn't tell me about it, sir,' he said. 'But there wasn't much they could do, was there now?'

'They seemed to regard the note as a practical joke,' said Michael.

'You must admit yourself, sir,' said Bartram, 'that it *did* look as if it might have been something of the sort. Of course, in view of what's happened since

— this dead man — it takes on a more serious aspect.'

'We'll probably get a line on the murderer when we've got the dead man's identity,' put in Sergeant Bishop confidently.

'I've an idea that you may have to go farther back than that,' said Hoppy.

'Farther back?' inquired Bartram, a little puzzled.

'To the murder of Helman,' answered the reporter.

'What on earth has that got to do with it?' interpolated Michael.

'William Crayle was the owner of this cottage,' said Hoppy.

'But that was, let me see, over six years ago,' said the chief inspector. 'I don't see how it could tie up with this business.'

'Neither do I,' said Hoppy. 'But Crayle's motive for the killing of Helman never came to light.'

'Well,' said Bartram, 'Crayle was hanged — there's no mistake about that — so he can't have had anything to do with this murder.'

'Don't forget the estate agent, Yardle,'

said Michael. 'His extraordinary disappearance is only another mystery.'

'We've been inquiring into that, sir,' said Bartram, 'and you are right about it being mysterious. There's no trace of him anywhere, neither him nor his car.'

'I shouldn't have thought it would have been very easy to conceal a car,' said Michael.

'If you can conceal a motorbike, you can conceal a car,' said Hoppy.

The chief inspector gave a sharp glance.

'Meaning in the same way?' he asked.

'Why not?' asked the reporter. 'In my opinion, Yardle's dead.'

'Have you any reason for saying that?' asked Bartram quickly.

'No reason that you'd call evidence,' said Hoppy. 'It's just a hunch.'

'You're suggesting, Mr. Hopkins,' said Bartram, 'that there's a connection between this disappearance and the death of this other man?'

'Don't you think so?' asked the reporter.

The chief inspector pursed his thin lips.

'I haven't come round to thinking yet,' he answered candidly. 'There may be, and there may not be. We'll be in a better position to judge when we learn the identity of the dead man.'

But the identity of the dark-haired man, only served to make the mystery surrounding Bracken Cottage deeper still.

7

It was Hoppy who first learned what the dead man's name had been. It came in a long telegram that was delivered on the following morning.

The reporter came into Michael's study with this fresh information.

'They've traced the number of the motorbike,' he said. 'The chap's name was Larkin, Richard Larkin, commonly known to his friends as 'Tich'. He had a room over a small café in Soho.'

'How do you know it's the same man?' asked Michael.

'Because they've checked up on the description I sent,' retorted Hoppy. 'There are no flies on the *Messenger*, I can tell you. Tich Larkin has been living in Soho for over eighteen months. He was mixed up with quite a number of crooks and unsavoury characters, always seemed to have plenty of money, but nobody can say where it came from.'

'Are you going to pass the information on to Bartram?' said Michael.

Hoppy shook his head.

'There's no need,' he said. 'He's probably got it himself by now.'

'Well, it doesn't get us very much farther, does it?' said Michael. 'We don't know what this fellow Larkin was doing here.'

'Rome wasn't built in a day,' answered Hoppy cheerfully. 'Have a bit of patience. One step at a time is the motto of Bob Hopkins, Esquire. There's something pretty big behind this business.'

Michael sighed.

'The whole thing's a confounded nuisance,' he grunted. 'I wish to goodness it could be cleared up quickly, and then we could settle down in peace.'

The chief inspector arrived later on that morning. As Hoppy had predicted he had also received information regarding the dead man's identity.

'I've asked Scotland Yard to find out all that's known about him,' he said. 'Perhaps it'll give us a line as to what he was doing in the district. By the way, Mr.

Wayland,' he added, 'tell your wife not to be alarmed if she sees any men about the place. I'm having the woods and surrounding country searched.'

He didn't say what for, but they guessed he had taken a tip from Hoppy and was looking for Yardle's car.

Bartram had hardly gone when they received another visitor, and a completely unexpected one.

She arrived on a rather decrepit-looking bicycle, a middle-aged woman with a hatchet-shaped face, and a thin-lipped, determined mouth.

'You've got an advertisement in the paper for someone to do the cleaning,' she said to Ann's surprise. 'I've come after the job.'

Ann invited her into the kitchen. This seemed almost too good to be true. Of course, it wouldn't be true when the woman heard what had happened there . . .

'Quite a nice kitchen,' remarked the newcomer, looking round sharply. 'When would you like me to start?'

'Well — ' began Ann, but the woman

interrupted her before she could get any farther.

'I can fetch my things and start this afternoon,' she said, in a brisk, business-like voice, 'if that'll suit you. I should want one evening off a week, and Sunday afternoons. What are you paying?'

Ann, feeling rather swept off her feet, mentioned a sum.

'That'll suit me,' said the woman, nodding her head.

'I think I ought to tell you — ' said Ann, but again the woman broke in before she could finish.

'About the murder?' she inquired. 'I read all about it in the paper this morning. That's what decided me to come. I love murders. Detective stories and thrillers, I revel in 'em.' Her eyes sparkled with relish. 'I've never come up against a real one before.'

Ann concealed her astonishment with difficulty.

'In that case, Mrs . . . ?' she paused.

'Biter,' said the other. 'And it's not Mrs. — It's Miss.'

'Oh,' said Ann. 'Well, Miss Biter,

perhaps you'd like to see your room . . . ?'

Miss Biter agreed, and Ann took her upstairs and showed her the room they had set aside for the purpose. She appeared to be quite satisfied. On the way back downstairs, she said:

'I can do plain cooking, if you wish, and I'm quite good at gardening. I noticed that the garden could do with a bit of tidying up. By the way, I live at Camsford. I've got a room there at present. Now, unless there's anything else you want to talk to me about, I'll go back and pack my things. You won't object to my keeping my bicycle here?'

Ann wouldn't have objected to anything. Miss Biter seemed to her to be next door to a miracle. When she'd gone, Ann went in search of Michael and told him all about her.

'It's just unbelievable,' she declared. 'I'm sure I shall wake up and find it's all a dream. She didn't even mind the murder. In fact, she said it was because of that that she took the job.'

'It seems to be a remarkable bit of luck,' said Michael. 'It's one of our problems solved, at any rate.'

Chief Inspector Bartram would have been glad to have achieved even that modicum of success. His hope that the identity of the dead man would give him a lead, petered out that evening. Coming back to his office at Havershot police station, he found a quiet, well-dressed man awaiting him. He introduced himself as Detective-Inspector Grantham of the C.I.D., New Scotland Yard.

He had come, he explained, on account of Bartram's inquiries respecting Tich Larkin. He would be pleased if the chief inspector could arrange for him to see the body.

Bartram, rather surprised that he should have come all the way from London for this purpose, took him over to the mortuary.

All that remained of Tich Larkin lay on a marble slab covered with a sheet.

Grantham gently turned the sheet back so that he could see the face, which had been washed clean of the mask of dried blood that had disfigured it.

'Do you recognize him?' asked Bartram.

The other nodded slowly.

'Yes, I'm afraid I do,' he answered. 'Poor Larkin.'

His astonishment showed in the chief inspector's eyes.

'He was one of our men,' explained Grantham, replacing the sheet carefully. 'You've heard of the Ghost Squad?'

Bartram nodded.

'Larkin was one of 'em,' said Grantham. 'We've got a lot of men doing the same sort of job. They go and live among the crooks, become friendly with 'em, sometimes they even become one of them. Nobody knows that they're connected with the police. They're even unknown to the uniformed branch and the C.I.D. They're only known to me. They pass on any information that they get hold of to my special department, and that information has enabled us to prevent many planned robberies, or apprehend the perpetrators of others. They carry their lives in their hands, as you can guess.' He looked at the sheeted figure on the slab. 'Sometimes, they don't carry them long enough,' he added sadly.

'What was Larkin on to?' asked Bartram, and Grantham shook his head.

'I don't know, I wish I did,' he answered. 'It would help you to discover the person, or persons, who killed him, if we knew what he was working on. I suppose he stumbled on something and was following it up. There's no fixed rule about reporting to headquarters, you know. The Ghost Squad have a pretty free hand. They're bound to, if they're to be of any use.'

They walked back to the police station together, and after a cup of tea, Inspector Grantham took his leave.

'I should be glad if you'd keep what I have told you completely confidential,' he said as he shook hands at parting. 'So far as the public is concerned, the dead man was Tich Larkin with a not very savoury reputation. I've only told you what he actually was to save you, and your men, wasting your time.'

'I wish there was some way of finding out what he was doing down here,' said the chief inspector.

'Yes, it would save you a lot of trouble,'

said Grantham. 'I'm afraid there's not much hope of finding out, though.'

Bartram went back to his office, frowning thoughtfully.

* * *

Miss Biter arrived back at Bracken Cottage just after four o'clock that afternoon. She had arranged, she said, for her luggage to be brought by a carrier on the following day. Meanwhile she had brought with her, in a small holdall, all that was necessary for her immediate needs.

She produced from the holdall a clean white overall, which she put on, and immediately set about getting the tea.

Ann quickly discovered that she was neat and quick at her work. And she didn't talk.

When there was anything to say, she said it, and that was all. By the time dinner was over, Miss Biter had settled in so unobtrusively that she might have been living there for weeks.

'She's a find,' said Ann enthusiastically.

'A positive find. I do hope that nothing upsets her . . . '

Hoppy had gone up to town directly after lunch and he wasn't expecting to come back that night. He wanted, he said, before he left, to look up the details of the Helman murder. There might be something that would give him an inspiration.

It began to rain about nine o'clock and the wind got up, sighing round the house and sounding in the nearby woods like the waves breaking on a beach.

Miss Biter, after washing up the dinner things and tidying the kitchen, had gone up to her room. Except for the sound of the rain and the wind it was very quiet. Michael, his legs thrown over the arm of an easy chair, was reading a book. Ann, with her feet tucked up under her, sat on the settee, staring at the dying fire and considering a hot bath and bed. She felt very tired and she began to nod . . .

She woke up with a start to find Michael watching her with a quizzical smile. He had laid aside his book, and was smoking a cigarette.

'Time for bed,' he said, getting up. 'By

jove, listen to the wind.'

He went over to the window and pulled the curtains, staring out into the wet darkness.

'I'm going up to have a bath,' said Ann, rousing herself with a yawn. She got up off the settee and went over to Michael. With her hand on his shoulder she, too, looked out into the darkness. There was nothing to be seen, the garden, the surrounding woods, the whole countryside seemed plunged into a thick, impenetrable blackness

Michael was on the point of dropping the curtain when, suddenly, away in the woods facing them, sparkled a pinpoint of light. It shone steadily for a moment, winked, went out, and then began to shine on and off intermittently.

Ann caught her breath.

'What's that, Michael?' she breathed.

'I don't know, I'm looking at it,' he said.

The light continued to shine, sometimes just a short flash, sometimes a longer one.

'Somebody's signalling,' exclaimed

Michael suddenly.

'They're using the Morse code!'

'But,' began Ann, and he stopped her quickly.

'Don't talk, darling,' he said, and intently watched the little flashes of light in the darkness as they came and went irregularly,

'*I — am — here*,' he spelt out slowly,

'Is that what it says?' inquired Ann.

'Yes — over and over again,' said Michael. He made up his mind suddenly. 'Stay here, darling. I'm going to see who is sending that message . . . '

He turned away abruptly and almost ran into the hall for his raincoat. Ann followed anxiously.

'No, don't go, Michael,' she pleaded. 'Don't! It might be dangerous.'

'I'll be careful,' he promised, pulling on the coat. 'But I'm going to find out who is out there, and who he's signalling to.'

In spite of her protests, he unlocked the back door and slipped out. A storm of wind and rain lashed at him as he set off across the garden in the direction of the light. It was very dark and he found it difficult going. Twice he stumbled over the stones edging the flowerbeds and very nearly went sprawling in the mud.

At last he reached the fence that separated the garden of Bracken Cottage from the beginning of the wood. If he had judged rightly the light should be straight ahead. But there was now no sign of it. Everywhere was black as pitch.

Michael stopped and listened.

There was no sound but the howling of the wind and the hiss of the falling rain. Yet somewhere in the darkness the person who had signalled '*I am here*' must still be there. He wouldn't have had time to get away.

Michael strained his ears. Still no sound except the wind and the rain.

And then he heard a sound. But it was *behind* him.

He turned quickly, peering into the darkness. But the rain was beating into his face with the force of the wind, stinging his eyes and partially blinding him. But he could hear someone approaching.

The footsteps were half-stumbling and half-running . . .

A light went on suddenly in one of the upper windows of the house, shining out across the garden, and by its faint illumination, Michael caught sight of a dim figure coming towards him.

It was Ann!

Michael ran towards her and caught her by the arm.

'What did you come out for?' he whispered. 'Why didn't you stay in the house, as I told you?'

'I was afraid,' she gasped. The wind caught her hair and blew it in long, wet strands across her face. She hadn't waited to put on a coat and he felt her shivering with cold.

'You'll be in bed with 'flu, if you're not careful,' he said. 'Come along, we'll go back.'

Still holding her arm, he began to make his way back to the house. They had to fight against the wind and arrived both wet and dishevelled.

In the kitchen they found Miss Biter. She had put on her raincoat over her pyjamas and wore a scarf tied round her head.

'Is anything the matter?' she asked as they came in and shut the back door.

'No, it's all right, Miss Biter,' said Michael. 'We saw a light out in the wood and wondered what it could be.'

'Did you find out what it was?' she asked.

Michael shook his head. Ann had flopped into a chair. She was very wet. The heavy rain had soaked her almost to the skin, even in the short time she had been out.

'You'd better have some hot coffee,' said Michael, 'with a good dash of whisky in it, and get straight to bed. Go and get your wet things off.'

'I'll make some coffee,' said Miss Biter, practically, and set about it immediately.

Ann, still shivering, went upstairs, and Michael, taking off his soaked raincoat, went into the dining room and warmed his cold hands at the dying fire

For all the good he had done, he thought, he might just as well have stayed indoors. But there *had* been somebody out on the fringe of the wood, and their reason for being there on such a night must have been urgent. What had the message meant? '*I am here*'. Who was here, and who had the message been intended for? Was there somebody else lurking round the house in the darkness and the wind and the rain?

Ann came down with a warm dressing gown over her nightdress. Her hair was still damp but she was no longer shivering. She sat down, stretching out her slippered feet to the fire.

'*Did* you see anything out there?' she asked.

'Not a thing,' said Michael. 'The person, whoever it was, had stopped signalling by the time I got there.'

'I wonder what it meant — 'I am here',' said Ann frowning. 'Who could they have been telling they were there to?'

Miss Biter came in with a tray of coffee. She set it down on the low table before the fire, and paused as she reached the door.

'Is there anything more I can do?' she asked.

'No, thank you,' said Ann.

The gaunt woman wished them both

'goodnight' and went out, closing the door behind her.

Michael looked at the closed door with a thoughtful expression on his face. That message, twinkling through the darkness, had not been intended for either himself or Ann, and there was only one other person in the house.

Was it possible that it had been intended for the efficient Miss Biter?

8

Hoppy's first call, when he reached London, was at the imposing offices of the *Daily Messenger* in Fleet Street. Mr. Cowper, the news editor, a dour and disillusioned man, with a bald head and a permanent expression of discontent, greeted him without any outward signs of enthusiasm.

'Well,' he remarked in his rasping voice, which sounded as if his vocal cords were composed of sandpaper, 'You appear to have fallen right into it.'

'Call me lucky,' said Hoppy, grinning at him.

'There're a lot of things I'd like to call you,' grunted Mr. Cowper, leaning back in his chair, and surveying his littered desk with acute aversion, 'but you seem to have got on to something this time.'

'There's a big story in it,' declared Hoppy. 'I want a chit to the cashier.'

'You always want a chit to the cashier,'

Hoppy. 'The case was never completely cleared up, was it?'

'The murderer was found, convicted, and executed,' said the superintendent. 'What more do you want?'

'Were *you* satisfied?' demanded Hoppy.

Hallows looked at him thoughtfully.

'What are you getting at?' he asked after a pause.

Hoppy pulled up a chair and sat down.

'I'll tell you,' he said, and proceeded to relate all that had taken place at Bracken Cottage. He included everything, and Hallows listened in silence until he had finished.

'Very interesting,' he remarked, gently scratching his chin. 'Why do you think any of this has anything to do with the Helman murder?'

'The cottage belonged to Crayle,' said Hoppy.

Hallows raised his rather thick eyebrows.

'I know, but Crayle's dead,' he said, 'so I don't see how *he* can have anything to do with it . . . '

Hoppy fished a Woodbine out of his

pocket and lit it.

'Look here,' he said, 'I've got a hunch that the motive for Helman's murder is somehow mixed up in it. You never found out what it was, did you?'

The superintendent shook his head slowly.

'No,' he replied.

'Tell me,' said Hoppy, 'all you know about Helman.'

'That's a pretty tall order,' said Hallows with a wry smile. 'Lew Helman was a crook; there wasn't much that was crooked that he hadn't been mixed up in. His last job, before Crayle shot him, was that big mailbag robbery. Over two hundred thousand pounds they got away with, mostly in pound notes that were being transferred from one bank to another branch — '

'Who was in with him on that?' broke in Hoppy.

'A man called Pat Sullivan an' a feller known as 'Curly'. His name's Topp, that's why they called him Curly.' Hallows sighed. 'Childish, isn't it? Sullivan got seven years and Curly got six. They should be out now, if they got the full remission for good conduct.'

'When were they arrested?' asked Hoppy.

'About six months after Helman was killed,' answered the superintendent. 'Lew would have been pulled in, too, if Crayle hadn't shot him.'

'You charged them with the mailbag robbery?' said Hoppy.

Hallows nodded.

'How did you get on to 'em?'

'We got tipped off by an informer,' said the superintendent. 'They'd been talking. They will do it, these fellows. It's vanity — that's what catches 'em more often than not . . . '

'And you never recovered the money, did you?' said the reporter.

'No,' said Hallows, 'that vanished completely. None of the three had it, or any part of it, so far as we could find. It's my opinion the other man had it . . . '

'The other man?' repeated Hoppy quietly. 'Who was he?'

'Ah, now,' said the superintendent, pursing his lips. 'I wish I could answer that. There's a lot of people in this building who'd like to answer that.'

'Come on,' said Hoppy. 'Don't go all round the mulberry bush. What do you mean?'

'In the past ten years or so,' explained Hallows carefully, 'there've been quite a few big jobs done. Not petty little robberies, but big raids on banks and jewellers shops involving many thousands of pounds, you know that. Now, our people have thought for a long time that there was somebody at the back of all these jobs who did the planning. We've got a hint of him now and again, but that's all. That's the feller I mean by the 'other man' — Mr. King . . . '

'Is that his name?' asked the reporter.

'That's the name he was known by,' corrected Hallows. 'It was better than calling him 'Mr. X' although it meant the same thing.'

Hoppy leaned forward excitedly in his chair.

'Hallows,' he exclaimed, 'could this 'Mr. King' have been Crayle?'

'I see what's in your mind,' said the

superintendent, 'but there's no evidence to support it. We went pretty thoroughly into Crayle's history at the time he was arrested. Until he shot Helman there was nothing against him at all. He lived quietly in that cottage of his at Bracken Bottom, spent very little money — he hadn't very much to spend — '

'Where did he get what he did have?' interrupted Hoppy.

'His father left him a certain amount,' said the superintendent, 'mostly invested in a building society. From this he drew a small income — only a few hundred a year . . . '

'He could still have been the unknown 'Mr. King',' said the reporter. 'How did he work?'

''Mr. King'?' said Hallows. 'That's something I can't tell you. Nobody seems to know. We haven't any real evidence that he ever existed . . . '

'But his name was mentioned,' said Hoppy. 'There wouldn't have been any mention of a 'Mr. King' unless he had existed.'

Hallows shrugged his shoulders.

'Even that's not certain,' he answered. 'You know how it is? Somebody starts a rumour and it spreads. As said, we got a hint or two about him — nothing definite . . . '

'Well, for the sake of argument,' said Hoppy, 'let's take it that he not only existed but that he was Crayle. Now, if all these robberies, as you say involving many thousands of pounds, were planned by him, what happened to the money?'

Again Hallows shrugged his shoulders.

'That's something else I can't tell you,' he said. 'It's been puzzling us for a long time. You know as well as I do that we mostly catch these chaps after they've pulled a job because they're suddenly flush with money and start spending it right and left. One minute they're broke and the next they're chucking fivers about like waste paper . . . '

'But that didn't happen in these cases?' said Hoppy.

The superintendent shook his head.

'All the same, they got away with the money and the jewellery, or whatever it was,' continued the reporter, 'and it must have gone somewhere — '

'If you've got it into your head that it's cachéd somewhere in Crayle's old cottage,' broke in Hallows, 'you're barking up the wrong tree. That place was searched with a fine toothcomb, after his arrest, and there wasn't so much as a bent penny.'

There was nothing more to be got out of Hallows, and Hoppy took his leave. Coming out of the entrance to the Yard, he turned up Whitehall and walked to Piccadilly Circus. Halfway along Shaftesbury Avenue, he turned down Wardour Street and found himself in Soho.

In a small and narrow street there was a café, distinguished from all the other cafés in the district by a flamboyant painting of a group of palm trees, under which huddled half a dozen people who were obviously intended to be Arabs, round a rather emaciated-looking camel. To justify this pictorial representation on the window, the name 'The Oasis' had been inscribed in flaming red letters above it.

Hoppy knew the proprietor of The

Oasis very well indeed. He had been instrumental in doing Mr. Cellini a service three years previously, which the Italian had never forgotten. His daughter, Rosa, a pretty girl of eighteen, had got herself mixed up with an attractive, rather flashy man, who had completely turned her head. She refused to listen to anything against him and there were constant rows between herself and her father over this infatuation. It was Hoppy who had opened the girl's eyes to the nature of this undesirable acquaintance, by proving that he had a wife and two children whom he had callously deserted.

Rosa had come to her senses in time, and Roberto Cellini was so grateful to the reporter that he was always a welcome visitor at The Oasis and the little flat above the café where the Cellinis' lived.

Cellini was serving at the snack bar inside the entrance when Hoppy came in. His round face with the large, liquid-brown eyes, lit up with a smile as he recognized his visitor.

''Oppy,' he greeted with obvious

pleasure, 'it is a long time since you come 'ere, yes?'

'Been busy,' said the reporter. 'How are things, Roberto? Good?'

The Italian shrugged his plump shoulders.

'Not good — not bad,' he said. 'What would you like? Coffee?'

Hoppy was never allowed to pay for anything at The Oasis. Cellini would have been deeply hurt if he had offered to.

'Coffee,' he replied, and when the other had set the coffee in front of him. 'Can you spare a minute, later, Roberto? I'd like to have a word with you in private.'

He glanced round at the crowded tables at which sat a heterogeneous collection of humanity, some flashy, some shabby, but all stamped with the same furtive-eyed shiftiness.

'We go up to the flat,' said Cellini. 'I send for Enrico to take over.'

He pressed a button under the counter and presently a little, bald-headed man with a scar running down the side of his right cheek, appeared through the door at the back of the counter.

'I go upstairs with my friend,' said Cellini, removing his white apron. 'You take my place for a little, eh?'

Enrico nodded. He put on the white apron, which was much too large for him, and smiled at Hoppy.

Enrico — nobody knew what his other name was — had once been a member of a race gang. He had been badly injured in a razor fight and when the gang was broken up by the police, had been persuaded by Cellini to come and work for him. He occupied a tiny room in the flat above, kept the place clean with the assistance of Rosa, and acted as a kind of general handyman. He was devoted to both Cellini and his daughter, and showed no signs of wishing to return to his previous rather uncertain and precarious livelihood.

Cellini led the way through the door at the back of the counter and up the narrow flight of uncarpeted stairs. There was another door at the top, which gave admittance to a tiny hall.

'We go in here, eh?' said Cellini, opening a door on the left of the hall.

'Rosa is out shopping. We not be disturbed.'

They entered a small and comfortably furnished sitting room. Cellini switched on an electric fire and pulled forward an armchair.

'Sit down, 'Oppy,' he said. 'You like a drink?'

Hoppy shook his head.

'No thanks, Roberto,' he answered. He took out one of his inevitable Woodbines and lit it. 'I want you to help me, if you can.'

'Anything I can I always do for you, you know that, 'Oppy,' said the Italian.

'You get to hear of a lot of things,' said the reporter. 'Have you ever heard mention of a 'Mr. King'?'

Cellini nodded.

'I hear of him,' he said.

'What have you heard?' asked Hoppy.

Cellini shrugged his shoulders.

'Sometimes,' he replied, 'I overhear them when they are talking downstairs.' He stabbed with his finger at the floor. 'Little bits, you understand? I have heard them say the name, 'Mr. King'. But I do not know who ’e is. I have only heard his name.’

‘Have you heard it recently?’ asked Hoppy.

Cellini shook his head.

‘No,’ he answered. ‘I not hear it for one, two, three, six years . . . ’

‘Did you know Lew Helman?’ asked Hoppy.

‘Yes, he come in many times,’ said Cellini.

‘And a man called Pat Sullivan?’

Cellini nodded several times.

‘A big man, Irish,’ he said. ‘’E used to come with Helman and Curly. They not come any more. Helman dead. The other two in prison.’

‘You knew Curly Topp, too, did you?’ said Hoppy.

‘Yes. Both went to prison,’ said Cellini.

‘I don’t think they’re still in prison,’ said the reporter.

‘I ’aven’t seen them,’ said Cellini. ‘If they not still in prison they not been in the café.’

‘When they used to come here,’ continued Hoppy, ‘did they ever have anyone else with them?'

'No — just the three — on their own,' said the Italian.

'Can you remember whether it was one of them who mentioned 'Mr. King'?' asked Hoppy.

Cellini frowned.

'Maybe,' he said after a pause. 'I don't remember. So many come 'ere, you understand?' He looked at the reporter curiously. 'You on a story, 'Oppy?' he asked.

'I think I am,' answered Hoppy. 'I think I'm on a pretty big story, Roberto.'

'You be careful,' said Cellini. 'If it got to do with Sullivan an' Curly and they're not in prison, you be careful.'

'Like that, eh?' said Hoppy.

'Dangerous,' said Cellini. 'Very bad. You ask Enrico. He know.'

'That's a good idea,' exclaimed Hoppy. 'I never thought of Enrico. That was about the time he was mixed up with that race gang, wasn't it?'

Cellini nodded,

'I send 'im up to you,' he said, and went away.

Hoppy stubbed out his cigarette and lit another. If he could only find something to substantiate his hunch that the unknown 'Mr. King' had really existed, and that he and Crayle had been one and the same person, it would go a long way to solving the mystery of Bracken Cottage. He was convinced, in spite of Hallows's scepticism, that the queer series of events that had occurred down at Bracken Bottom was concerned with the proceeds of the mailbag robbery. The money might not be concealed in the cottage but he was beginning to be quite sure that the cottage was intimately connected with its present whereabouts. The thing he had to discover was whether Sullivan and Topp were at large again. If so, there seemed every likelihood that they were at the root of the whole business.

Enrico came quietly in.

'Boss says you want me?' he remarked, closing the door.

'I'd like to ask you one or two questions, Enrico,' said the reporter. 'Did you ever come across two men called

Sullivan and Topp in the old days?'

Enrico's face darkened.

'Yes,' he said. 'Very bad, very bad. Helman was another.' He made a gesture of disgust. 'Not stop at nothing . . . '

'What about 'Mr. King'?' asked Hoppy.

'What you know about 'im?' said Enrico quickly.

'Nothing,' answered Hoppy, 'but I'd like to.'

''E was behind the jobs pulled by Topp, Sullivan and Helman,' said Enrico. 'That's all I know about 'im.'

'That's more than most people,' said the reporter. 'They don't seem to be sure that he ever existed.'

Enrico came a little farther into the room. He rested his hands on the back of a chair and leaned forward.

'He existed,' he said quietly. 'Nobody ever saw 'im but he existed.'

'If nobody ever saw him, how can you be sure?' asked Hoppy.

'I 'eard Sullivan talking about him once,' answered Enrico. ''E was talking to Topp. In the Continental Espresso. They'd got a message to pick up the plans for a new job . . . '

Hoppy felt his pulses quicken. Was he going to learn something important at last?

'How were they going to pick up the plan without seeing 'Mr. King'?' he demanded. 'Oh, I suppose you mean he was sending a messenger?'

Enrico shook his bald head.

'No,' he said. 'He come himself. It was simple . . . ' He looked at Hoppy for a moment intently. 'You keep what I tell you to yourself?'

'I promise I won't say where I got the information,' said Hoppy.

'All right. That is good,' said Enrico. 'I have never said this before to anyone, you understand?'

Hoppy nodded.

'This 'Mr. King',' said the little Italian, 'used to telephone to a certain number — I do not know what it was — when he had a plan ready. He would arrange for one of those three to be at a certain place at a certain time — it was always at night, very late at night, and usually out in the country — a lonely road . . . '

Hoppy's eyes sparkled. Crayle had shot Lew Helman on a lonely country road near Basingstoke. Had he found a tangible link at last?

''Mr. King',' continued Enrico, 'would drive up in a car, with his face concealed — a handkerchief bound round it. The plan, all carefully written out and put in an envelope, would be handed over and 'e would drive away. It took' — he snapped his fingers — 'a few seconds, that is all. When the job had been carried out, another meeting was arranged — at a different spot, of course, always at a different spot — and the stuff would be handed over . . . '

'They must have been very trusting,' said Hoppy.

'It was safe, you understand?' said Enrico. 'If they were suspected, nothing could be found . . . '

Hoppy looked at him curiously.

'You seem to know a lot about it,' he remarked.

Enrico went to the door, opened it, and looked out quickly. Closing it he came back.

'The Boss does not know this,' he said lowering his voice. 'On one, two times, I followed them. Once Sullivan, once Helman. I saw what 'appened.'

'You saw 'Mr. King'?' exclaimed Hoppy, but the other shook his head.

'No,' said Enrico, 'only the car he drove . . . '

'The make?' asked the reporter, and again Enrico shook his head.

'It was too dark to see,' he said.

'You actually saw some of the proceeds of a robbery handed over?' said Hoppy.

'Yes.'

'What made you so curious?' said the reporter.

Enrico hesitated.

'I wish to find out — it was before I come to work for the Boss, you understand? I think there may be something to be made out of finding out . . . '

The bald-headed little man looked embarrassed, and Hoppy understood. Enrico had contemplated a little blackmail . . .

'Can you tell me anything else?' he asked.

'No, that is all,' said Enrico. 'I have not said it to anybody, you understand? It was soon after this that I was beaten up in the gang fight and came to work for the Boss. You won't say about it to 'im?'

Hoppy shook his head.

'I won't say anything to Roberto,' he promised. 'You don't know how you've helped me, Enrico.'

'The Boss's friends are my friends,' said Enrico. 'You once very kind to 'im. He very kind to me, so I kind to you.'

He smiled.

'I've got to find out whether Sullivan and Topp are out of prison,' said Hoppy. 'If they are — '

'Sullivan is,' broke in Enrico.

'How do you know?'

Enrico shrugged his shoulders.

'Because I saw him in Frith Street, one, two — three days ago,' he said.

9

The storm of wind and rain blew itself out during the night, and when Michael woke up on the following morning, a pale sun was struggling through thin clouds.

He looked out of the window in the direction of the spot where they had seen the light flashing. Now that it was daylight he could see that here the wood thinned to a straggle of trees. The signaller, whoever it was, had chosen a place giving an almost uninterrupted view of the house.

While he shaved and had his bath, Michael cogitated over the matter. Had the idea that had come suddenly to him on the previous night been right? Was the message '*I am here*' intended for the gaunt Miss Biter? It seemed more than likely. In which case, who was she, and what was her object? It certainly accounted for her presence, which had seemed so opportune.

Ann had said it was almost too good to be true that they had succeeded in getting a woman like Miss Biter. Perhaps she had been right. Perhaps Miss Biter had reasons of her own, reasons that she hadn't divulged for taking the job. There was no atom of proof, of course, that the message had been intended for her, but if the unknown signaller had been flashing his message to someone who was also outside, why hadn't he given it to them verbally? There was no need, surely, to flash a message in Morse code to someone whom you could quite easily, by walking a few yards, speak to personally? There was no need to flash a message at all to make your presence known in that case. The message was only necessary if it was impossible to speak to the person who was to receive it. And the only person who fitted was — Miss Biter.

Miss Biter, then, had taken the job in order to gain a legitimate admittance to Bracken Cottage. Why she should have done so was more than Michael could fathom. But then there was such a lot that he couldn't fathom. There was the disappearance of Yardle, the man with the measuring tape, the oiled gate, the note, and the dead man in the loft. If Miss Biter was there under false pretences, then she must be part of all these queer happenings — she must know all about the murder.

Michael wondered whether he ought to inform Bartram of his suspicions regarding her, and decided that he would consult Hoppy first. The reporter should be back some time that day, and a few hours couldn't make much difference.

But he made up his mind to keep a sharp eye on the gaunt woman from that moment.

By the time they had had breakfast, the sun had succeeded in completely dispersing the clouds, and was shining brightly. It wasn't warm, but it was cheerful.

Miss Biter was her usual efficient self. She made no reference to the event of the previous night, but went about her work methodically and quietly. It seemed almost impossible to believe that she had any other interest.

Michael wanted to finish a short story

that was due to be delivered to a magazine on the following day. There was not much of it to be done, and if he finished it that morning he could get it in the post soon after lunch.

'I've some shopping to do,' said Ann, when he told her his plans. 'If you're going to be busy, I'll take the car and drive into Havershot. I'll go early so I should be back by lunchtime. Is there anything you want?'

'Well, I'm nearly out of typing paper,' he said. 'You might get me a ream. Oh, and some cigarettes . . . ' he added.

Ann nodded and went upstairs to get her coat.

Michael saw her off and then went up to his study to work. He was so engrossed in completing the story that he never noticed the passing of time, and it was with a slight shock of surprise that he found it was nearly half-past twelve by the time he had typed the last word and sorted out the scattered sheets into a neat pile. He wrote a letter to his agent, enclosed the manuscript in a large envelope, sealed it down, and addressed it ready for posting.

Going downstairs, he found Miss Biter laying the table for lunch.

'No, Mrs. Wayland hasn't returned yet,' she said in reply to his question. 'She told me she'd be back for lunch, but it won't be ready for another fifteen minutes.'

Michael lighted a cigarette and went out into the garden. It was muddy and wet underfoot, but the sun was still shining, though a faint mist seemed to be gathering in the hollows of the woods. It was very cold and he soon returned to the warmth of the sitting room fire. Pouring himself a gin and french, he sat down to await the return of Ann and lunch.

But the time went by and there was no sign of Ann.

At the expiration of half an hour, Miss Biter came in to inform him that lunch was ready and what should she do about it? Would he have his? She was afraid it would spoil if she kept it hot any longer. He decided that he might as well have it. Probably Ann's shopping had taken longer than she had expected. They weren't on the telephone yet so she couldn't let him know if she'd been delayed. Quite likely she'd get some lunch in Havershot.

He ate his meal — an excellent one of lamb cutlets followed by a fruit salad and cream — in solitary state, and went back to the sitting room.

Two o'clock came and went, half past two, three, and still there was no sign of Ann.

At four, Michael began to feel uneasy. What on earth could be keeping her all this time? She might have met with an accident, the roads would be slippery after the rain . . .

Then he thought that perhaps she had run into Hoppy in Havershot. That might be it. And they had had lunch together . . .

By five o'clock it began to get dusk, and Michael was really feeling alarmed. So, to his surprise, was Miss Biter.

She didn't say anything, but when he went out to listen for any sound of an approaching car, he found her by the iron gate, staring anxiously up the narrow road.

There was no sound at all of anything approaching — nothing but the slapping of the sodden trees to break the stillness.

'I don't know what can have happened,' muttered Michael.

'I hope nothing has,' said Miss Biter.

There was a tinge of anxiety in her voice that made him look at her sharply.

'I don't see what can,' he said. 'She's a very good driver . . . '

The gaunt woman said nothing.

At six o'clock, Michael put on his raincoat and walked up the road leading to the cottage. It was the only way anyone in a car *could* come, but he reached the crossroads at the top without encountering a soul, either driving or on foot.

At the crossroads he hesitated.

The way to Havershot lay on his right — a long, deserted stretch that lost itself in the darkness and the thickening mist. And the mist was gathering rapidly, a white, opaque vapour that was creeping over the whole countryside, obliterating everything in its cloudy blanket.

What could have happened to Ann?

What was the best thing to do?

Michael felt helpless. What could he do? It was no good standing here staring into the mist. He felt a wave of complete helplessness come over him. Even if he could have got to Havershot, he had no means of finding Ann. There was only one thing to do, go home and wait. Maybe there was some good reason that had delayed her return.

He set off to walk back along the long road that led to the cottage. The mist was thick now. He could only see a few yards in front of him and he wished that he had brought a torch.

It was slow going, groping his way in the darkness and the swirling white vapour, but, after what seemed to him an age, he came at last to the iron gate.

He went in and up the short drive. He went round to the back of the house but the kitchen door was locked. He knocked but he could not make anyone hear. Probably Miss Biter was upstairs. He made his way round to the front door and opened it with his key. The hall was in darkness and so was the sitting room.

A comforting warmth, for he was

chilled to the bone, wafted out to greet him as he opened the door and switched on the light. The fire had burned low, and he stirred it to flames, putting on a log from the box at the side of the fireplace.

He took off his raincoat, and went out into the kitchen. The light, here, was on, and there was a kettle simmering on the gas cooker. He looked at his watch. It was nearly a quarter to eight.

No sign of Ann. No sign of Hoppy, either.

He went out to the foot of the staircase and called to Miss Biter.

There was no reply, and he ran quickly up the stairs and knocked at her door.

No answer!

He hesitated, and then opened it, peering in. The room was in darkness and fumbling for the switch, he pressed it down. As the light came on, he looked quickly round the room.

It was empty!

Hastily he made a search of all the rooms. They were all empty. Quickly he made a thorough search of the entire cottage.

Except for himself, there was no one there. He was alone in the house!

* * *

Hoppy had fully intended to return to Bracken Cottage after leaving The Oasis but the information he had acquired from Enrico caused him to change his mind.

He was feeling very elated with himself. His idea about Crayle looked like turning out correct. There was no reason at all why he shouldn't have been the unknown 'Mr. King', the brain behind the series of thefts and robberies carried out by Lew Helman, Pat Sullivan, and Curly Topp. In which case, there was a very sound explanation for the series of strange events that had taken place at Bracken Cottage.

If Crayle had been in possession of the proceeds from these various robberies and had concealed them in the cottage, there was an almost perfect explanation for all that had happened there.

With the exception of the disappearance of Yardle and the murder of Tich Larkin.

Those two items didn't fit in. Or did they?

As Hoppy saw it, something like this had happened. When Crayle had shot Lew Helman — the reason for that was another thing that required explaining — he had given himself away to Sullivan and Curly Topp that he was 'Mr. King'.' Even if they'd both been half-witted they must have guessed that. The fact that he had had a house at Bracken Bottom must also have been known to them. It had been in all the newspapers at the time of the trial. It didn't require much intelligence to guess, also, that it was in this house that he had hidden the proceeds of the robberies. It was a sitting duck. An empty house, all on its own, in the heart of the country. All they had to do was to walk in and search for a fortune.

Unfortunately for them, they had been arrested before they could do anything about it, and sentenced to long prison sentences. But during their time in prison they must have been planning eagerly for the time when they would be free and in a position to collect the fortune that awaited them.

And then, when they had at last come out, they had discovered that the cottage was occupied. This couldn't have been entirely a surprise, they must have expected something of the sort. Probably they had, and laid their plans to cover such an event.

This would account, thought Hoppy, for the man with the measuring tape, the oiled gate, and the note. What it did not account for was the disappearance of Yardle and the murder of Tich Larkin. Unless, of course, Larkin had got on to what they were up to and tried to horn in. That might explain it. But not Yardle.

Could that just be a coincidence? It might be that the estate agent had had a reason of his own for vanishing, a reason that had nothing to do with the rest of it.

Hoppy decided to leave the Yardle part of it alone for the time being. That left two things to be accounted for — the motive for the killing of Helman, and how Crayle, alias 'Mr. King', had persuaded such tough crooks as Helman, Sullivan, and Topp to calmly hand over all the loot to him. The only explanation for that, so far as Hoppy could see, was that he must have had some hold on them. The hold that instantly came to mind was that he knew them while they didn't know him. A word from him to the police would have shopped them. That's probably what he held over them and made them part up so easily.

But they couldn't have been very satisfied with the arrangement. Could that have been the reason for the Helman murder? Was Helman kicking at the traces?

Even without all these issues cleared up, Hoppy felt that he had gone a long way. The thing now was to find out just when Sullivan and Topp had been released and get hold of a photograph of both of them.

It was because he wanted to do this that decided him not to go back to Bracken Cottage until the following day.

Once more he presented himself at Scotland Yard, but this time he sent up his form to the Records Office.

'Collectin' pin-ups?' asked the inspector in charge when Hoppy explained what he wanted.

'Something of the sort,' answered the reporter.

'You couldn't call either of these fellers beauties,' remarked the other. 'You wait till you see 'em.'

He went away, returning after a short interval with two cards.

'Take a look at 'em,' he said with a grin. 'If their mother ever loved 'em she must've been easily pleased.'

Hoppy took a look at them.

Curly Topp, in direct contrast to his name, was very nearly bald. His face was thin and vicious-looking with small eyes that were set too near to a crooked nose. Sullivan had a face like a retired boxer. His mouth was thick and his jaw pugnacious. His eyes were staring and curiously dead-looking, like blank windows, and he possessed a mass of unruly hair.

'I suppose I can't have a copy of these?' said Hoppy, and the inspector shook his head.

'I'm afraid you can't,' he said.

'Do you happen to know,' asked the reporter, 'when these two came out of prison?'

'I don't,' answered the inspector, 'but if you hold on a minute, I'll try an' find out for you. Always willin' to oblige the Press, I am.'

He was gone for nearly twenty minutes.

'The chief inspector would like to see you,' he said, when he returned, 'Room 107. On the next floor.'

Rather surprised, Hoppy went in search of Room 107.

The man who sat behind the very orderly desk looked up as he entered.

'Come in,' he said unnecessarily because Hoppy was already in. 'You're Hopkins of the *Messenger*, aren't you?'

'That's right,' said Hoppy. 'I don't think I've met you before.'

Chief Inspector Motington shook his head.

'You haven't,' he said. 'But I've heard of you. Why are you making these inquiries about Sullivan and Topp?'

'I'm following up a story,' said the reporter.

'I though you probably were,' said the other. 'Well, I shouldn't follow it any farther, if I were you.'

'Why?' demanded the astonished Hoppy.

'You might become rather a nuisance if you do,' said the chief inspector. 'In which case, I should have to be firm about it, and I don't want to.'

'What exactly do you mean?' asked Hoppy.

Motington smiled.

'A nod is as good as a wink to a blind man, so they say,' he said. 'Lay off this business, there's a good chap.'

10

Ann was longer over her shopping than she had expected. It came as a surprise to her when she discovered that it was already past twelve when she had finished. She ought never to have stopped for a cup of coffee in that café attached to the stores. But she had felt terribly thirsty and dying for a cigarette.

She went in search of the place where she had parked her car and was just getting into it when she remembered that she'd forgotten to get Michael's typing paper. The shop was at the other end of the main street. Perhaps, if she were very quick, she could leave the car outside for a moment while she made her purchase.

There was no sign of a policeman in sight as she pulled up outside the shop, so she hurried in. Parking was strictly prohibited, but, to save time, she was determined to risk it.

She secured the paper and came out to

the car. She breathed a sigh of relief as she got in and drove away. Michael would have been furious if she'd been caught.

It was now nearly half past twelve and she would have to hurry to get back to the cottage in time for lunch. She put her foot down on the accelerator hard, as soon as she was clear of Havershot, and watched the needle of the speedometer climb steadily to fifty. She thought that was as fast as she dared go on the wet roads.

By the time she reached the crossroads and turned into the one that led down to Bracken Cottage, a glance at her wrist-watch showed the time to be ten minutes to one. She would just make it in time.

And then, ahead of her, she saw two men in the roadway. They seemed to be bending over a third who lay stretched out on the rutted surface.

Ann slowed down. As she did so one of the men turned towards her. He said something to his companion and ran towards the car.

'Excuse, miss,' he said as he came level with the window. 'There's been an accident. There's a fellow in the road there that looks as if he's been badly hurt.'

Ann opened the door of the driving seat and got out. It was a nuisance, since she was in such a hurry, but she couldn't very well ignore the matter. Anyway, she couldn't drive on. The man who lay in the road prevented that.

'Do you know who it is?' she asked.

The man who had spoken to her shook his head.

'No, miss,' he said. 'Me an' my friend found him like that. Been run over, by the looks of things.'

'But there isn't any traffic down this way,' said Ann. 'It only leads to my house . . . '

'Well, you see for yourself,' said the man.

They had reached the injured man by this time, and Ann bent down to look at him . . .

Something was whipped round her head and she took a deep breath of something that was sickly and pungent . . . She fought to try and get the enveloping blanket off but it was held firmly . . . Somebody's hands gripped her arms and forced them down to her sides . . . As her senses fled she felt herself being lifted up . . .

* * *

When her senses slowly came back to her, Ann's first sensation was one of physical sickness. The second was of a strong, musty smell with the acrid odour of decay. She opened her eyes, winced, and closed them again quickly. Even that slight action had sent a shooting pain through her head.

After lying quite still for a few minutes, she felt better. The sickness passed away and the pain was less intense when she opened her eyes. She could see nothing at all at first, and then she made out a few pale streaks of light. They seemed to be shining through the walls, or whatever enclosed the place she was in.

She tried to move her arms but they were fastened securely to her sides. And it was the same with her legs and ankles.

As her return to consciousness became complete, memory came flooding back. The man in the road . . . the two men bending over him . . . She had gone to see what was the matter, and then . . .

The cloth, or whatever if was, that had been flung round her head must have been soaked in some drug . . .

She'd been kidnapped!

The whole thing had been arranged. She remembered that what she had thought was a man lying in the road, hadn't been a man at all, only a dummy. She had seen that in the second before the obscuring cloth had blotted out everything . . .

But why should someone want to kidnap her?

Almost before the question had formed in her mind, the answer followed it. This was part of the other queer happenings that had taken place recently.

Her thoughts flashed to Michael. Had anything happened to him, too? Perhaps this was the result of ignoring the warning note . . .

Her eyes had been growing accustomed

to the gloom. What she had originally thought was total darkness, now seemed to be pervaded by a faint, dim glow. It came, she discovered, from the streaks of daylight that percolated through the planks that composed the walls. She was in some kind of a wooden building — a shed or a barn. It looked too small for a barn . . .

In the gloom she could make out some heaps of something that appeared to be stacked against the walls. It was from these heaps that the rotten smell came. The floor felt damp to her fingers, and, after groping about with her fingertips, she came to the conclusion that it was mud. There was a door in one corner — she could just make it out. It was probably locked, but if she could get free surely she could find something with which to prise it open, or rip some of the planks from the wall . . .

She tested the cords that bound her. They were pretty tight. They cut into the flesh even through the thick coat she was wearing. She strained and struggled to see if she could loosen them, but they wouldn't give the fraction of an inch. Whoever had done the tying had made a good job of it.

She lay still, panting for breath from her exertions. How far, she wondered, was she from Bracken Cottage? And what had they done, these unknown men who had brought her here, with the car? If they had left it in the road leading down to the gate, Michael would find it. Or somebody would find it. Whoever did would wonder what had happened to her. They would try to find her. But supposing they *couldn't* find her . . . ?

She felt panic begin to surge up inside her. She might lie here, helpless, for days — even weeks. She would starve . . .

She renewed her struggles to free herself until she was completely exhausted. It was no good. The cords had been bound too tightly. Try as she might, she couldn't loosen them . . .

She lay still, listening for any faint sound that would tell her where she was. But there was no sound at all. Everything was as still as the grave . . . She shivered. It might very well be her grave . . .

The panic within her increased. She tried to scream but her dry throat only enabled her to utter a strangled sound that would not have penetrated outside the shed . . .

What was the meaning of it all, she wondered? Why had this happened to her? What object was there in making her a prisoner in this place?

The two men had been strangers to her. The first was a big, burly man, with a heavy face. The other was slighter. She had been unable to see his face — he had kept it turned away from her . . .

Her thoughts turned again to Michael. What was he doing? Had something happened to him, too? If he were still at the cottage, he would become terribly worried when she didn't return. But there wasn't much he could do . . . Perhaps he would go to the police and there would be a search for her . . . But would they find her? That depended on where she was . . .

She was feeling hungry and dreadfully thirsty. She would have given anything for a drink of water. Her lips were dry and her throat felt parched. It was most likely due to the drug that had been on the cloth they had thrown over her head . . .

She tried yet again to see if she could loosen her bonds, but the effort brought on a splitting headache that made her temples throb as though her head was full of miniature hammers, and she had to stop.

What could she do? There must be something she could do. She couldn't just lie here and die . . .

Did anybody ever come here? What was the place used for? To whom did it belong? But it wasn't much use thinking about that. The men who had brought her here would never have chosen the place unless they were certain that she wouldn't be found . . .

The time dragged slowly by. The streaks of light between the planks that formed the walls of her prison began to fade. Soon they had gone altogether and there was nothing but darkness. The pain in her head eased a little but her eyes felt heavy and hot. She closed them and drifted into an uneasy sleep . . .

* * *

Michael came slowly back to the sitting room. There was no doubt about it. The house, except for himself, was deserted.

He poured himself out a stiff whisky and drank it neat. The glow of the spirit ran through his veins and helped to steady his nerves.

What had happened to the gaunt woman? Why had she gone and where had she gone? To meet the signaller who had flashed the message '*I am here*'?

This had all been carefully planned. Something had been done to keep Ann away. He was desperately worried about that. What had been done? Had she been injured?

Michael paced up and down the sitting room with an anxious and troubled face. There was a cigarette in his fingers but it had gone out. The little clock on the mantelpiece ticked steadily on. It was nearly a quarter past eight

A smell of burning metal sent him into the kitchen The kettle had boiled dry on the gas cooker and was nearly red-hot. He turned off the gas, picked up the kettle with a dishcloth and put it in the sink. It occurred to him as he did so that surely, if Miss Biter had intended to go, she wouldn't have left the kettle boiling? But perhaps she had forgotten it.

He opened the back door and looked out. The fog had grown very thick. Swirls of opaque white vapour enveloped the house. It was impossible to see more than a couple of yards. That deadness, which is one of the chief characteristics of fogs, hung palpably in the air, like an enveloping blanket. The world and everyone in it might have suddenly ceased to exist.

Michael shut the door again and turned the key. Bracken Cottage lay completely isolated in that obscuring, damp mist — cut off from civilization as effectually as if it had been built on a desert island.

And he was alone.

It was not a pleasant thought considering all things. He had little doubt in his mind that something was going to happen. All that had happened before had simply been the prelude to this . . .

What would happen he hadn't the remotest idea. Whatever it was he couldn't do anything about it. There was no telephone here — there was no means of communication with the outside world at all.

Michael went back to the sitting room and put more coal on the fire, stirring until it blazed cheerfully. The clock on the mantelpiece ticked on. Slowly the hands moved round until they pointed to nine o'clock.

What could have happened to Ann?

This was the main thought that kept worrying him. If only he knew. Where could she be, out in that impenetrable fog?

He wished with all his heart that Hoppy had been there. Why hadn't he come back, either? What had happened to everybody?

Half past nine.

Everything was very silent. There was no sound outside, no sound inside, except the ticking of the clock and the faint noise made by the burning coal.

He lighted a cigarette and tried to force himself to think, calmly and clearly. If Ann had met with an accident of any sort he would have heard, The police would have notified him. She had plenty in her bag to identify her. He remembered that she had got him to type out her name and the address of Bracken Cottage to put in her wallet. So even if she had been severely injured, he would have heard. That practically ruled out an accident. That left two alternatives. Either she was staying away of her own accord, or she had been forcibly prevented from coming back.

He could think of no possible reason for her staying of her own accord. She couldn't have run into friends. Neither of them knew anybody in the neighbourhood. She might have met Hoppy in Havershot, if the reporter had come back from London as he had said he was going to, but that wouldn't have kept her all this time.

There remained only the latter of the two alternatives — that she had been forcibly prevented. But who would want to do that? Michael passed a weary hand across his forehead. That was impossible to answer. All the series of queer events that had taken place were, he was sure, working up to something — something that was planned to happen at Bracken Cottage — but who was responsible for the planning he'd no more idea than the man in the moon.

An owl hooted outside the house.

The eerie, hollow screech sounded fairly near. Michael's nerves tautened. He had no idea what might happen, but all his senses were keyed up for something Ten o'clock.

Perhaps, he thought wearily, he would have to sit up all night. In any case, without knowing what had happened to Ann, it wouldn't be possible to go to bed. There was no chance of his sleeping.

The owl hooted again. This time the sound seemed farther away. Where could Miss Biter have gone in the fog? He wondered if she had taken her bicycle. There wasn't much sense in going out in the fog and the cold to look. What did it matter whether she'd taken it or not? She was gone, that's all that mattered.

But curiosity eventually got the better of him. He had to know whether that bicycle was there or whether it was gone.

He found his torch, went out into the kitchen, and unlocked the back door. The fog was so thick now that it formed a wall of white close up to the door that looked almost solid.

Michael stepped out into it. It was bitterly cold — a raw chill that struck through to his marrow. He made his way carefully round to the outhouses at the side of the cottage, in one of which Miss Biter had kept the bicycle. The torch was practically lifeless. Its ray failed to penetrate the fog to any appreciable extent. He could see nothing at all but the white vapour that hemmed him in on all sides. The cottage had vanished. It might never have been there. He thought, grimly, that if it had vanished it would only be on a par with all the rest of the queer things that had happened, and almost as unexplainable . . .

He found the outhouses at last. It seemed to have taken him hours. He opened the door of the one where the bicycle should be and flashed his light inside.

It was still there.

The gaunt woman hadn't gone on her bicycle then. But surely she wouldn't have walked in this weather if she had gone any distance? The fog hadn't been so bad at the time she must have gone. But if she hadn't gone a considerable distance, where was she? She couldn't be lurking in the woods or somewhere close at hand, in this raw cold, unless she'd gone suddenly stark, raving mad. Even that possibility, thought Michael, wouldn't have surprised him. Nothing would have surprised him. If he returned to the house and found that it was completely different to the one he had left, he wouldn't have been surprised.

But everything was the same when he got back. The fire was burning cheerfully, the clock was still ticking away on the mantelpiece. He went over to the drinks table and poured out a Johnnie Walker. The cold outside had left him shivering. He drank half of it and carried the remainder over to the fire.

Half past ten.

11

Hoppy caught the nine-forty-three train back to Havershot on the following morning. He had got most of the information he had come to London for, and a bit more into the bargain. His idea concerning Crayle and 'Mr. King' seemed to be right, but he was a greatly puzzled man all the same.

And the thing that puzzled him was the attitude of Chief Inspector Motington.

He had been, very tactfully it was true, warned off.

'We don't want you to play in our backyard.' That's what it amounted to. Keep off the grass.

There was only one explanation for this. Scotland Yard was playing a little game of its own and they didn't want Hoppy interfering.

Well, that was all very well — Hoppy had no intention of annoying the powers that be. They had been too useful in the past, and were likely to be so again in the future, for him to be silly enough to do that. But he wasn't going to keep out of it altogether. He'd have to move warily, and, of course, keep what he had discovered to himself.

The train pulled into Havershot Station and, getting out, Hoppy made his way to the station approach and looked round for Michael. He had sent a wire on the previous night saying what train he was catching. The wire should have reached Bracken Cottage that morning in time for Michael to pick him up. But there was no sign of him.

Perhaps the wire had been delayed. You could never rely on things getting there to time in the country.

Hoppy waited for twenty minutes and then, when there was still no Michael, he went off to find some means of being conveyed to the cottage. He found a garage that ran a hired car service and arranged to be driven to Bracken Cottage.

He dismissed the driver at the iron gate and walked briskly up the short drive to the house. There was no reply to his ring at the front so he went round to the back. The back door was locked. Hoppy hammered on it for several minutes but nobody answered.

They must be all out, he thought. Going to the veranda, he peered through the french window into the sitting room. It was quite deserted and the fire was out.

Hoppy frowned.

Where was everybody? Had they all gone shopping? Surely they wouldn't have taken Miss Biter with them?

He tried the window and found that it was unlatched. That was something, anyhow. He wouldn't have to hang about in the cold. The fog of the previous night had gone but there was a heavy frost. He opened the window and entered the sitting room, shutting the window behind him. The air was warm but not so warm as it would have been if the fire had been alight that morning.

Hoppy felt the grate. It was stone cold. There had been no fire in it that morning. He was puzzled. Something must have happened, but what?

And then he saw the note.

It had been propped up against a vase on the top of the low bookcase. It was typewritten and read:

'Had to go up to town on business. My wife has gone with me.' It was signed with the initial 'M'.

So that was it, thought Hoppy. Oh well, he'd have to make himself as comfortable as he could until they came back. Michael hadn't mentioned when that would be. He hadn't said anything about Miss Biter, either. What had happened to her? Perhaps they had given her the day off.

He went in search of wood and paper and lit the fire. When that was burning, he took off his overcoat and poured himself out a drink. Lighting one of his inevitable Woodbines, he sat down in an easy chair and relaxed.

What should be his next move? Queer, Michael hadn't put 'Ann' instead of 'my wife'. What had taken him up to London in such a hurry? He might have said when he was coming back. Probably knew I'd make myself at home until he does, thought Hoppy. He switched his mind back to the problem that was occupying it.

There was little doubt, he thought, that in some way or other Bracken Cottage held the secret of what Crayle had done with all the loot. Perhaps it was hidden somewhere actually in the place. The police had been over it with a small toothcomb at the time, according to Hallows, but they hadn't been looking for hidden treasure.

Or had they?

After his interview with Chief Inspector Motington, he could not be sure what the police knew. Most likely they'd worked it out on the same lines as he had.

He looked at the clock. The hands pointed to ten minutes past three. It couldn't possibly be as late as that. He glanced at his watch. No, it was barely a quarter past two. The clock had stopped. He got up and looked at it. It had stopped because it hadn't been wound.

Curious, thought Hoppy, as he wound it up and put it right. It wasn't like Michael to forget a thing like that. He was very methodical in most things. He must have been in a tearing hurry to get away . . .

Hold on, though. The clock had stopped at ten minutes past three. Was that yesterday afternoon or in the small hours of the morning? It couldn't have been yesterday afternoon. The clock wouldn't have run down by then. Michael, then, had forgotten to wind it last night.

Hoppy made a grimace. He was trying to make something out of nothing. He had no idea when Michael and Ann had left . . . It might have been yesterday or the day before. There was no date on the note.

The reporter began to feel hungry. He went out into the kitchen to see what he could find in the way of food. He discovered some cold meat and tomatoes in the pantry with the remains of an apple pie. He had a good meal, felt considerably better, and made some coffee.

There were signs that the fog was coming down again with the setting of the sun, but as yet it was fairly clear.

It was just after three when the bell

rang. Hoppy went to the front door and opened it. A woman stood on the step. She was a middle-aged woman, wrapped in furs, and her face was seamed and wrinkled.

'Good afternoon,' she said in a voice that was low and melodious, not at all in keeping with the ugliness of her face. 'I'm Mrs. Newsome. Is Mr. Wayland at home?'

So this, thought Hoppy, was Crayle's sister.

'There's nobody here but me,' he answered, and introduced himself. 'Mr. and Mrs. Wayland have gone up to London. Won't you come in?'

Mrs. Newsome hesitated.

'I just thought I'd call and see how they were getting on,' she said. 'I've been over to Havershot on business. I don't think I'll come in . . . '

'I'm sure you'd like a cup of tea,' said the reporter. 'I was just going to make one for myself . . . '

'That's very kind of you, Mr. Hopkins,' she said. 'I should love a cup of tea. But I can't stay very long. I want to get home before this horrible fog gets any thicker. It was terrible last night.'

Hoppy took her into the sitting room and she looked round with interest.

'They've certainly made a very nice place of it,' she remarked. 'I'm sorry to have missed them. I seldom come out, but I thought this would be a good opportunity. You're staying with them, are you?'

'For a short while,' said Hoppy. He went out into the kitchen and put the kettle on. When he came back, Mrs. Newsome had loosened her furs and removed her gloves.

'Did you say you were a reporter on a newspaper?' she asked.

Hoppy said that he was, and she seemed interested. She asked him several questions about his job and whether he was staying at Bracken Cottage because of the murder. 'It was really a dreadful thing,' she said. 'I felt so sorry for Mr. Wayland and his wife when I heard about it.' She sighed. 'It really seems that this house must have some kind of attraction for violence. You know that it originally belonged to my brother, William Crayle?'

Hoppy nodded.

'I'm really very glad that it no longer belongs to me,' she went on. 'I do hope that there won't be any more trouble here.'

'I hope so too,' said Hoppy, but remembering what he had discovered about Sullivan and Topp his tone sounded a little dubious. She was quick to notice it.

'But you think there might be?' she said. 'What makes you think that, Mr. Hopkins?'

Instead of answering the question, Hoppy put one of his own.

'How well did you know your brother?' he asked.

'Latterly, not well at all,' she answered. 'We scarcely ever met although we were living in the same district. Why do you ask that?' Her eyes were sharp and curious.

Acting on an impulse, Hoppy told her his theory. She listened, her bright eyes fixed on his face, and when he had finished, she said:

'I've no means of judging whether you're right or wrong. William may have been this man 'Mr. King'. But it seems to me a little far-fetched to suppose that the stolen property is hidden somewhere in this house. Where do you imagine it to be?'

'I don't know,' said Hoppy. 'It would have been very well concealed.'

She smiled a trifle grimly.

'It would have to be,' she retorted. 'I suppose you are aware that the police searched this place very thoroughly after the murder? If there had been anything of the sort, surely they would have found it?'

'Not necessarily,' replied the reporter. 'Without pulling the whole building down, it would be impossible to be certain.'

Her eyes glinted with amusement.

'Are you going to suggest doing that to Mr. Wayland?' she asked. 'Having just bought the property, I shouldn't think he would like the idea at all.'

'There might be other ways of finding it,' said Hoppy.

'Always supposing that there is anything to find,' she answered.

Hoppy left it at that. Quite obviously

Mrs. Newsome rather discounted the suggestion that there was anything to find. But something had happened to the proceeds of the mailbag robbery and the other jobs that had been carried out by Helman, Sullivan, and Curly Topp. None of the stolen stuff had ever been discovered and, therefore, it must be somewhere. Bracken Cottage seemed to Hoppy to be the most likely place.

They had tea, and Mrs. Newsome rose to go.

'Give my regards to Mr. and Mrs. Wayland,' she said as he accompanied her to the door. 'And let me know how you get on with the treasure hunt, won't you?'

He heard the sound of her car drive away, shut the door, and returned to the sitting room. He sat down and lighted a Woodbine. Mrs. Newsome hadn't taken his suggestion seriously, but he was convinced that he was right. Somewhere in the house was the accumulated loot from all these robberies. Could he find it?

There was no harm in having a try. He had the place to himself. Why not occupy his time in searching? Where would be the most likely place? If he had been Crayle where would he have chosen to hide the stuff?

He was considering this when the door began to open slowly. He didn't notice it at first, and then, as he caught sight of it out of the corner of his eye, he jumped up from his chair and swung round.

Miss Biter stood on the threshold. And in her hand was an automatic pistol.

12

Michael Wayland stirred uneasily and opened his eyes. His head hurt him horribly, as though the whole of it was one large, throbbing bruise, and he couldn't see anything but blackness. For a little while he lay still. He felt stiff and uncomfortable but when he tried to move he found that this was impossible. His dazed brain groped to find a reason and eventually he discovered that his arms and legs had been tightly bound.

Memory came back in queer little jerky pictures . . . The fog-bound house and his search for Miss Biter's bicycle . . . pouring himself out a Johnnie Walker . . . the warmth of the fire . . . the clock pointing to half-past ten. Something had happened after that . . . He had never drunk all the whisky. *What* had happened . . . ? What *had* happened . . . ?

Now he remembered. The haze was clearing . . . Queer . . . it was as though that thick fog had somehow got into his brain . . . He had heard a noise . . . in the kitchen. He had gone to see what it was and that was all he remembered . . .

Where was he now? Still at Bracken Cottage? No, he couldn't be. There was a queer smell in his nostrils . . . There hadn't been any smell like that at Bracken Cottage — a nasty, fusty smell — a smell of rottenness.

It was bitterly cold, too — cold and damp . . .

He was lying on his back but he managed to turn over on his side . . . His cheek came in contact with a cold and clammy substance, and he could smell the odour of damp earth . . . Where on earth was he? He seemed to be lying on something muddy . . .

A faint sound attracted his attention. It came from somewhere quite near — a soft sound that at first he couldn't place . . . And then it came to him. It was somebody breathing!

So he wasn't alone in this place, whatever it was. There was somebody else there, too . . .

He tried to call. At first his dry throat refused to function, but at the second attempt he managed to speak. It was a husky, hoarse sound, quite unlike his usual voice.

'Who's there?'

The sound of breathing stopped.

'I'm — I'm Ann Wayland,' answered a weak voice, but clear and recognizable. 'Who are you?'

'Ann!' he answered. 'Ann . . . It's . . . Michael . . . '

There was an exclamation in the darkness.

'Michael! So those men got you, too . . . ?'

'Yes . . . Where . . . is this . . . this . . . place?' he asked.

'I don't know . . . It's horrible. I've been here a long time . . . '

'What happened?' he said. 'Tell me what happened, Ann . . . '

She told him.

'You're not hurt?' he asked anxiously.

'No. My head still fells funny — like cotton wool,' she replied. 'What happened to you?'

He told her as much as he could.

'Somebody must have come in while I was looking for the bike,' he ended. 'As I came out of the sitting room, they hit me on the head . . . '

'I heard them bring you here,' said Ann, 'but I didn't know who it was. They threw a cloth over my head — so that I shouldn't see, I suppose. I don't know when it was. I've lost count of time . . . '

'Are you tied up like me?' he asked.

'Yes. I've tried hard to loosen the cords, but I couldn't.'

'I'll have a go at mine,' he said. 'It's lucky they didn't gag us.' He paused to recover his breath. 'Look here, I'll see if I can roll over towards you. If I can find the knots, I might be able to untie them . . . '

He tried to put this plan into practice, but he didn't get very far. After rolling over and over with great difficulty for a little way, he came up against a barrier of some kind.

'There's something in the way, Ann,' he said breathlessly. 'I can't get any farther.'

'They were hauling something about after they brought you in,' said Ann. 'I suppose that's what it was. Oh, Michael, I'm so hungry.'

'We've got to get out of this,' said Michael. 'Have you tried shouting?'

'Yes, but I don't think it's much good,' she said. 'I couldn't shout very loud. My throat's so dry . . . '

'If I ever get hold of the men who did this,' said Michael angrily. 'I'll make them wish they'd never been born.'

'Have you any idea who it could be?' she asked.

'No, I suppose it's mixed up with all the other things,' he said. 'What were the two men like who stopped you?'

She described them as best she could.

'The other man — not the one who spoke to me, but the other — I think he was the man with the measuring tape,' she said. 'I couldn't be sure . . . '

'Well, they told us there'd be trouble if we didn't clear out,' said Michael. 'Now, they've cleared us out . . . '

'I wonder what happened to Miss Biter?' said Ann.

'I don't care what happened to her,' answered Michael. 'I'm only interested in what's going to happen to us. She's probably in this business, too . . . '

'Hoppy'll do something when he comes back and finds the place empty,' said Ann, hopefully.

'But he may not be able to find us,' replied Michael. 'We've got to get out of this, darling, somehow. Let's shout . . . '

'Nobody will hear us if we do,' said Ann. 'It must be the middle of the night. You can tell when it's light, it shows through the planks.'

Michael was silent for a minute. Ann was right. It wasn't any good wasting energy shouting unless there was a chance that somebody would hear. There couldn't be much chance of that or they would have been gagged. Where the dickens were they? It was no good wondering about that. They might be anywhere.

As Ann had said, Hoppy would be alarmed at their absence, but what could he do? Go to the police? But what could they do? There was the car, of course. But that would have been hidden somewhere too. Unless the men who'd brought them here released them they might stay indefinitely — perhaps forever.

Michael shuddered.

Did anyone ever come to this place? What was it used for? From the mouldy smell it seemed to be some kind of store. But it couldn't be much in use or there wouldn't be that smell of rottenness. It was like decaying grain of some kind . . .

'When the light shows through the chinks in the walls, can you see?' he asked.

'A little,' she replied. 'Only very dimly.'

'If I could see,' said Michael, 'there may be a way round this barrier, whatever it is. If I could get to you, I could at least try to undo those knots.'

'I wonder how long it'll be to daylight?' she sighed.

'We'll just have to wait patiently until it comes,' said Michael . . .

* * *

The fog came down with the dusk. It began in the woods and hollows, and crept stealthily nearer and nearer to

Bracken Cottage, rising as it moved until it had enveloped the house completely.

If anything, it was thicker than the previous night. By the time darkness had fallen the house and everything else was completely obscured in a cold, clammy white mist that was like steam. Some giant boiler of nature might have opened its safety valve except that the temperature was near freezing-point.

There was no sight or sound of life in the house itself. It was dark and deserted, sprawling in the heart of the mist like a great dead animal. There was no sight or sound of life either in the surrounding woods, or in the sodden garden, or in the road that led to the rusty iron gate. It was as if the world had died and been already committed to a shroud.

Somewhere, muffled by the fog, which deadens all sounds, a clock struck the hour of eight. As it ended, the silence was broken by the sound of a car engine. It came slowly down the road, moving at a crawl, its lights making little impression on the white mist that swirled and eddied in front of them.

Eventually it reached the iron gate and stopped. The vague figure of a man got out, felt his way to the gate, and opened it. He uttered a faint whistle, and the car moved forward again. It passed through the gateway and up the short drive, coming again to a stop in front of the house.

The first man had followed it on foot and when he reached it he was joined by another, smaller man who had been driving.

'Couldn't have had a better night, Pat,' he remarked, his breath steaming and mingling with the mist.

'We should have the place to ourselves,' grunted the man addressed as Pat. 'Let's get inside out of this infernal fog, Curly. It gets in your throat.'

'Maybe we'll find a drink inside,' replied Curly Topp. 'I could do with a good stiff whisky. I'm frozen to the bone.'

'You can lay off that,' snapped the other. 'Come on.'

He moved off towards the back of the cottage, stumbling now and again over the uneven ground, and cursing softly when he did so. They came to the veranda and mounted the shallow steps.

'You got the torch?' asked Pat Sullivan, as they paused outside the french window.

Curly Topp drew it out of his pocket.

'Shine it near the lock,' said his companion. 'There's one thing, we don't have to be quiet on this job. I don't suppose there's anyone else for miles.'

'Except Wayland and his missus,' said Topp, switching on the torch and directing its light on the lock of the window.

'They're safe enough,' grunted Sullivan. He took something from his pocket and there was a tinkle of glass. He put his hand in the hole of the smashed pane and twisted back the catch. A pull and the window opened.

He stepped inside, followed by the other. In contrast to the freezing atmosphere outside, it felt warm, and he grunted again with satisfaction.

'That's better,' he said. 'Shut the window, Curly, and draw the curtains. I'll put the light on.'

Topp did as he was bid, and as the light came on, sending a soft warm glow over the room, he spotted the bottle of Johnnie Walker on the drinks table.

'That's me,' he said. 'We'll have a warmer before we get busy.'

'You go easy on that stuff,' warned Sullivan. 'We've got a long job before us . . . '

'I'm only going to have one,' said Curly, going over and pouring himself half a tumbler of the spirit. 'Going to join me?'

'I don't mind one,' said Sullivan. He looked round the room. 'For years I've dreamed about being here,' he said. 'All those years in 'stir', I've thought an' planned for this moment. During the long hours when the lock was on, I've thought of the time when I'd be free an' pick up a fortune . . . '

Curly handed him a drink.

'We've still got to find it,' he said, swallowing half his whisky at a gulp. 'That isn't going to be so easy,'

'We'll find it,' retorted Sullivan confidently. 'We've got plenty of time.

Nobody's likely to disturb us — now.'

'Where are you going to start?' asked Topp. 'The stuff may be anywhere. You don't know where he put it. It may not even be in the house. It may be buried somewhere outside, for all you know.'

Sullivan took a sip of whisky and shook his bullet head.

'It'll be inside,' he said. 'Maybe down in the cellar, if there is a cellar. We'll start at the bottom an' work our way up.'

Curly Topp helped himself to a cigarette from a box on the low coffee-table in front of the dead fire.

'Everything provided,' he remarked as he lit it. 'All the comforts of home, eh? This is the sort of job I like.'

He finished his drink and cast a longing eye at the bottle.

'You can take your eyes off that,' snapped Sullivan. 'You've had all you're going to have until we've finished the job.'

'Well, let's get started then,' said Topp.

They went out into the hall. There was a door under the side of the staircase that looked as if it might lead to the cellar. Sullivan opened it and peered in.

'Here we are,' he said. 'Give me that torch, Curly.'

He took the torch the other held out to him and flashed the light into a dark void in which was a narrow flight of stone steps that led downwards. He descended them, followed by his companion, and they found themselves in a small, whitewashed cellar.

There was very little in it, a few boxes, a stack of firewood. That was all.

'I wonder where they keep the coal?' remarked Topp.

'They've got bunkers outside the back door,' grunted Sullivan. 'You ought to know that. Don't you remember 'em?'

Curly made no reply. He was eagerly scanning the walls and the concrete floor.

'It doesn't look as if there was any place here he could've hidden the stuff,' he said. 'Unless he buried it under the concrete or bricked it up in the walls.'

Sullivan shook his head.

'He wouldn't've done that,' he declared. 'He'd have put it somewhere that was easily get-at-able . . . '

'It's not down here, then,' said Curly. 'I

shouldn't think the walls or the floor had been disturbed since they was laid.'

'I think you're right,' agreed Sullivan. 'We'll go back upstairs.'

They went back up the narrow flight to the hall. Sullivan put on the light and looked round.

'You'd better go easy with the lights,' said Curly Topp. 'If anybody spots 'em, it's not going to be so good.'

'It wouldn't be so good for them,' grunted Sullivan grimly.

'You've done enough killing, Pat,' said his companion.

'I've only done what I had to do,' retorted Sullivan. 'I couldn't let that 'busy' feller get away, could I? He spotted me when I was having a look round the joint. I didn't know he was a split until after I'd croaked him. If he'd gone back and told about seeing me here, the cops would've put two an' two together, wouldn't they? They knew this place belonged to Crayle — '

'But they didn't know Crayle was 'Mr. King',' interrupted Curly.

'They knew he shot Lew, an' they knew

that Lew was mixed up with us,' snapped Sullivan. 'They're still looking for the stuff, Curly, don't forget that,'

'It was a pity that other chap saw you kill Larkin,' said Topp.

'It was a pity for him,' said Sullivan.

'It was a pity for both of us,' corrected Curly. 'It started people wonderin'.'

'Well, he wasn't found, was he — or the car,' said Sullivan, 'and it'll be a long time before they are. I drove it well out of this district. That tunnel on the disused railway line made a good hiding place . . . '

'It's a swinging matter if you get pinched,' said Curly.

'And for you as well, don't forget that,' said Sullivan. 'You were in it as well as me.'

'You did the killing,' said Topp.

'That doesn't matter — not in law,' retorted his companion. 'You're just as guilty as what I am, an' you'd better not forget it.'

'I'm not forgetting it,' said Topp. 'That's why I want to get out of here as soon as possible . . . '

'We're safe enough,' said Sullivan. 'But we may as well get on with the job. Once we've got the stuff, we'll be away an' out of the country before they can pin anything on us. Let's go back to the sitting room. I've a fancy that might be the place.'

They went back, and Sullivan stared slowly round the room.

'That panelling looks promising to me,' he said, after a pause. 'Let's have a shot at sounding it. You take that wall over there, and I'll take this one. If you strike a spot that sounds different to the rest, give a shout.'

He drew a clasp-knife from his pocket and began methodically tapping the old panelled wall, while Curly Topp did the same to the other wall. But they only got a solid sound. There was not the faintest suggestion of there being a hollow space behind it anywhere.

'Now we'll try the other walls,' said Sullivan.

'Couldn't we just have a spot first?' said Curly, looking at the half-full bottle of Johnnie Walker.

'No,' snarled Sullivan. 'Once we've got

what we came for, you can drink yourself to death, if you like, but you're not touching any more now.'

Topp looked sullen but he said nothing. They repeated their previous operations on the other two walls and with a similar result.

Sullivan straightened up and wiped his face.

'There's nothing here,' he grunted. 'We'll try the hall. That's panelled too.'

'What about this other room here?' suggested Topp, jerking his thumb at the door of the drawing room as they came out into the hall.

'We can try that after the hall,' said Sullivan.

'I suppose you haven't forgotten that the place has got floors?' said Curly.

'We'll try the walls first,' answered Sullivan. 'I'd say they were the more likely.'

They adopted the same procedure with the walls of the hall and up the oak staircase. Nothing.

'This looks like being a long job,' grumbled Topp.

'I wish we had some sort of clue . . . '

'Well, we haven't,' snapped Sullivan irritably. 'We always knew it'd be a long job. That's why we went to so much trouble to get the house to ourselves.'

The drawing room yielded nothing either. The painted walls were solid. There was not the faintest indication of any hollow space behind them.

'Short of pulling the whole place down brick by brick, I don't see how we're ever going to find it,' said Curly discontentedly. 'Maybe it isn't here at all — '

'It's here somewhere,' broke in Sullivan. 'Where else could he have hidden it?'

'Anywhere,' answered Topp.

Sullivan shook his head.

'He'd keep it under his eye,' he said. 'We'll try the bedrooms. And then we'll go over the whole place again. I'm going to find it.'

Topp looked at his watch.

'It's already past midnight,' he said.

'So what?' demanded Sullivan. 'If it takes us all night it'll be worth it — '

'If we find it,' finished Curly pessimistically.

They mounted the stairs to the bedrooms.

'We'll start with the main bedroom first,' said Sullivan, opening the door and switching on the light. 'You take that wall, I'll try this.'

It was Curly who made the first discovery. The fireplace had been filled in and a panel electric fire installed. Over the chimney-piece, the wall, when he tapped it, sounded hollow. He called to Sullivan.

'This sounds as though there might be a space behind it,' he exclaimed excitedly.

'Probably only the chimney,' said Sullivan. He came over and looked up at the wall. Like the rest of the room, it had been divided into oblong panels outlined by wooden beading. The panels themselves had been painted a pale lilac, the spaces between being white, like the rest of the paintwork. There was only one panel over the fireplace, and when he tapped it, there was certainly a hollow sound.

Sullivan felt the wooden beading carefully. It seemed solid enough. He took a screwdriver from his pocket and inserting it between the wall and the beading at the bottom of the panel, wrenched it off.

And then he uttered a triumphant exclamation.

'We've got it, Curly,' he cried. 'Look!'

Where the wooden beading had come away was a thin line. With his face alight with excitement, Sullivan attacked the remaining three sides of beading. When it was removed, the whole panel was revealed to be a close-fitting door. So close did it fit that the crack round its edges was scarcely visible. With the wooden beading in place it was completely undetectable.

Sullivan drove the point of the screwdriver into the thin interstice and prised it open. The door swung on almost invisible hinges. Behind it, almost filling the entire space, was the door of a safe.

'We've got it!' cried Sullivan.

He reached up and tugged at the handle of the safe's door. But it refused to budge. It was locked. But they had come provided for such a contingency.

'Let's get the 'cutter' out of the car,' said Sullivan. 'We'll have that safe open in a jiffy.'

They almost ran down the stairs through the kitchen, and out into the fog. In the back of the car was the oxy-acetylene apparatus. They carried it in between them and up to the bedroom.

'Better get some water, just in case,' said Sullivan. 'We don't want to set the place on fire . . . '

While Curly, full of excitement, went to get the water, Sullivan got the oxy-acetylene apparatus going. Adjusting the burner, he carefully turned on the gas — the mixture of oxygen and acetylene that produced such a heat that the flame would cut through steel like a hot knife through butter.

'Curly' came back with a jug of water, as Sullivan put on a pair of smoked glasses.

'Better not look,' he warned, as he mounted a chair and sent the flame impinging on the door of the safe. There was a blinding light and a shower of brilliant sparks as the flame bit into the steel and ate its way round the lock. After a few minutes, Sullivan switched off the burner and handed it to Topp.

'Now,' he cried exultantly, and pulled open the door of the safe.

It was empty!

13

Sullivan uttered a cry of disappointment mingled with rage. Curly Topp stared at the bare interior of the safe with disbelieving eyes.

'Empty!' he muttered. 'Empty!'

Sullivan glared at the empty safe with eyes that had become suffused with blood from suppressed anger.

'Who could have got it?' he demanded. 'Nobody could have even guessed it was there but us . . . '

'Perhaps the police found it?' suggested Curly.

If there had ever been anything in the large safe there was nothing now. Not so much as a scrap of paper. It was a wide, shallow, steel compartment, set in the chimney, and tightly cemented round. A steel shelf divided it in half.

'What do we do now?' inquired Topp.

Sullivan, still staring at the empty safe as though by the very intensity of his gaze he would fill it with what he had desired, made no reply.

'There's not much we can do, is there?' Curly went on. 'We may as well pack up and go . . . '

Sullivan swung round on him with an oath.

'You did this,' he accused, 'You were out before me. You came down here and cleared out the stuff . . . '

'What do you mean?' broke in Topp angrily. 'I haven't been near the place . . . '

Sullivan rushed at him and caught him by the collar.

'You're lying!' he shouted, his face suffused with rage. 'You're lying, you double-crossing swine! Only you could have — '

'Let me go,' cried Topp, gripping the other's thick wrists and trying to break free. 'I'm not lying . . . '

Sullivan shook him like a terrier with a rat.

'What have you done with it?' he cried. 'When did you find it . . . ?'

'I tell you I haven't found it,' panted

Curly. 'Let me go, will you . . . ?'

But Sullivan only transferred his grip to Topp's throat.

'I'll squeeze the life out of you,' he said between his teeth.

Curly's face turned purple. His tongue protruded as the merciless grip tightened, choking him. He lashed out with his foot at Sullivan's ankles, but his spasmodic efforts missed. He heard a roaring in his ears and a crimson curtain, flecked with flashes of orange, rose up before his eyes. He felt himself growing weak, but there was no relaxing of the grip on his throat. And then:

'That'll do, Sullivan!' snapped an authoritative voice from the door.

Sullivan swung round, releasing his grasp of Topp.

A big man stood in the open doorway. Behind him, Sullivan could see other men . . .

Curly staggered to the bed and fell on it, gasping for breath, his hands clawing at his throat.

'I want you, Sullivan,' said Chief Inspector Motington. He came farther into the room, followed by Chief Inspector Bartram and Sergeant Bishop. Two plainclothes constables brought up the rear.

Sullivan's hand flew to his hip pocket, but before he could pull out the automatic he was searching for, Motington sprang forward and gripped his wrist. The two plainclothes men rushed forward to his assistance and Sullivan was secured between them. Even then he fought like a demon, but he was quickly overpowered and they got the handcuffs on him.

'Get that man too,' ordered Bartram, jerking his head towards Curly Topp, who was still drawing in great wheezing breaths on the bed.

There was no fight left in Curly after his gruelling at the hands of Sullivan, and they had no difficulty in securing him.

'We've been waiting for you, Sullivan,' said Chief Inspector Motington. 'We thought when you came out of prison you'd lead us to the stolen property . . . '

Sullivan gave a harsh laugh.

'You can have all you can find and

welcome,' he said. 'See that?' He pointed at the safe with his manacled hands. 'There it is — *all* of it.'

'Somebody got there before you, eh?' said Bartram. 'Well, it wouldn't have done you much good, or Topp either. You're charged with murder . . . '

'The murder of Richard Larkin,' put in Chief Inspector Motington softly. 'Do you mean that you found this safe empty?'

'As old Mother Hubbard's cupboard,' retorted Sullivan He had gone suddenly quiet after his previous outburst, as though he had decided to accept the inevitable.

'He accused me of taking it,' croaked Curly Topp hoarsely. 'He'd have killed me if you hadn't come . . . '

'Saved the hangman a job,' said Bishop.

'Had you taken it?' asked Chief Inspector Bartram.

Curly shook his head.

'No,' he answered. 'I don't know anything about it — I swear I don't. I was as much surprised as he was . . . '

Chief Inspector Motington frowned.

'Somebody else must have known

about it, if you're speaking the truth,' he said.

'The only people who knew about it was me, Curly an' Lew Helman,' put in Sullivan, 'and Helman's dead.'

'You're forgetting Crayle,' said the chief inspector.

'Crayle's dead, too,' said Sullivan. 'He was hanged.'

'I know that,' snapped Motington. 'Why did he kill Helman?'

'I don't know,' said Sullivan surprisingly. 'I've always wondered.'

'You knew Crayle was 'Mr. King', didn't you?' asked Motington.

'Not until after he'd shot Lew,' said Sullivan. 'We knew then, because Lew had had one of the usual messages to meet 'Mr. King' . . . '

There was a commotion in the corridor outside and Hoppy burst into the room. He was followed by the gaunt Miss Biter.

'He wouldn't stay out of it — ' she began, but the reporter interrupted her.

'No, I won't,' said Hoppy, angrily. 'Look here, that's Michael Wayland's car outside. What happened to him? What's happened to his wife . . . ?'

'You'd better go and look,' snarled Sullivan,

'They're all right,' put in Curly Topp. 'We didn't hurt 'em.'

'Where are they?' demanded Hoppy, but Sullivan shut his teeth.

'Come on,' snapped Bartram. 'What have you done with Mr. and Mrs. Wayland?'

'Find out!' retorted Sullivan.

'This won't help you,' said Motington.

'I'm not asking for any help, am I?' said Sullivan. 'You can only hang me once, so what's the odds — '

'I'll tell you,' broke in Curly, and Sullivan shot him an angry glance,

'Why you white-livered swine!' he began, but Bartram cut him short.

'That'll do from you!' he said sharply. 'Bishop — you go with Grey and get Mr. and Mrs. Wayland . . . '

'Yes, sir,' said Sergeant Bishop.

'I'll come with you,' put in Hoppy.

Bartram turned to Curly.

'How far away are they?' he asked.

'Only about half a mile,' said Topp. 'We

put 'em in the old hut in the wood . . . '

'Come on, then,' said Sergeant Bishop. 'I hope you can find your way in the fog.'

Accompanied by Hoppy and one of the plainclothes men, he and Curly Topp went downstairs. Miss Biter went to the head of the staircase to see them on their way.

'You'd better get this fellow away,' said Chief Inspector Motington, nodding at Sullivan. 'Think you can manage to get him to Havershot tonight?'

'Oh, yes,' said Bartram. 'We'll have to go slow, but we'll be all right in the police car. I know this district pretty well. I could find my way blindfold.'

'That's about what you'll have to do,' said Motington with a smile.

'Are you coming with us?' asked Bartram.

The chief inspector shook his head.

'No,' he replied. 'I'll stay and have a word with the Waylands.'

'What happened to the stolen property?' asked Miss Biter, who had come back into the room.

Motington shrugged his shoulders.

'Your guess is as good as mine,' he said. 'There's no sign of it.'

The gaunt woman frowned.

'My employers aren't going to be too happy about that,' she said.

'I'm not too happy about it, either,' said Motington, 'but there's nothing I can do. I banked on the fact that Sullivan would lead us to it, and I was wrong . . . '

'It must have been here,' said Miss Biter, looking at the empty safe. 'Who could've taken it?'

Motington shook his head.

'I don't know,' he said. 'We'll go into that later.'

Bartram and the other plainclothes man took Sullivan away. The man went quietly enough but there was a glint in his eyes, which they failed to notice.

In the kitchen, Bartram slipped his hand into his prisoner's hip pocket and took out the automatic.

'I'll take charge of that,' he said, and dropped it into the pocket of his overcoat.

The fog was just as thick and they had difficulty in making their way even the short distance to where the police car was waiting outside the iron gate. Both kept a wary eye on Sullivan in case he tried to make a dash for it.

It took Bartram some time to bring the car in and turn it round, but he managed it at last. Sullivan and the plainclothes man sat in the back seat. It wasn't easy going. Bartram had to drive at a snail's pace because of the fog, but eventually they negotiated the road up from Bracken Cottage and came to the crossroads at the top. Bartram took the road that led to Havershot. It was a fairly straight road, and, as he had said, he knew every inch of the way. He increased their speed slightly. Farther on there was a patch where the fog had thinned a little. It may have been that Bartram, taking advantage of this, increased the speed too much, or it may have been that there was an icy film to the surface of the road where the rain had collected and become frozen. Whatever was the cause, the car suddenly skidded badly, and before Bartram could correct, had spun round and landed in the ditch that ran alongside the road at this point.

The jolt flung Bartram forward so that his head came in contact with the instrument board in front of him. It wasn't a bad blow but it dazed him for a moment. The plainclothes man in the back with Sullivan, was jerked sideways against his prisoner, striking his head badly against the frame of the window.

Sullivan instantly took advantage of the accident.

He threw open the door, almost fell out of the car, and vanished in the fog.

Bartram saw him go, yelled to his companion, who was dizzy from the blow on his head, and struggled to get out from behind the wheel. He succeeded, but it was a minute or so before he was standing in the roadway, trying to decide in which direction Sullivan had gone.

* * *

Sullivan stumbled on through the thick white mist, cursing the handcuffs on his wrists, which hampered his movements. After a short while, he stopped, panting for breath and listening. There was no sound of pursuit and he thanked his lucky stars for the fog. He went on again after a short pause, stopped again to listen, and then sat down behind a hedge at the side of the road. With difficulty he took the screwdriver from his pocket, which he had used to remove the beading round the concealed door at Bracken Cottage, and set to work to try and 'spring' the lock that fastened the handcuffs. Sullivan was an expert at locks, and although it took him the best part of an hour, he succeeded at last and flung the handcuffs away.

He was quite free now and he knew exactly what he was going to do. With luck he could get clear away. If he could reach his objective without getting caught, he would be safe.

For he knew where he could find both sanctuary and the money.

It had come to him suddenly, while he had been talking to Chief Inspector Motington.

A few more hours and he would have the stolen property in his possession . . .

* * *

A fire roared halfway up the chimney in the sitting room at Bracken Cottage. Before it sat Michael, Ann, Hoppy, and Chief Inspector Motington. Miss Biter, who had made quantities of hot coffee to restore her two half-frozen employers back to life, sat primly on a chair at the back of the small circle.

Sergeant Bishop, and Grey, the plain-clothes man, had borrowed Michael's car to transport Curly Topp to Havershot.

'I don't think I'll ever be really warm again,' said Ann with chattering teeth, holding out her numbed hands to the grateful warmth of the fire. 'It was awful in that shed. Damp and cold, and I was so hungry and thirsty . . . '

'You had longer of it than I had, darling,' said Michael. 'What you ought to do is to go to bed with lots of blankets and a couple of hot water bottles.'

'I'm going to get thoroughly warm first,' she said. 'Can I have some more coffee, please?'

Miss Biter got up, poured out another

cup of coffee, and handed it to her.

Hoppy eyed the gaunt woman curiously.

The biggest surprise he had ever had in his life was when he had seen her standing in the doorway of that room with the automatic pistol in her hand. Everything else had come as an anticlimax . . .

'I don't think you'll have any more trouble here,' said the chief inspector. 'We've been waiting for years to get Sullivan and Topp. Unfortunately, we haven't got the stolen property which was our objective.'

'If you knew it was here — ' began Michael, but Motington interrupted him.

'We didn't know where it was,' he said. 'But we knew it must be somewhere. We calculated that Sullivan and Topp would be after it as soon as they came out of prison, and we arranged to have them tailed — that means watched,' he explained with a smile as Ann looked at him inquiringly. 'Topp was the first out, but he made no move so we waited for Sullivan . . . '

'Is that why you were so anxious that I should lay off?' asked Hoppy.

The chief inspector nodded.

'I didn't want you to scare the birds,' he said.

'But you must have known that Crayle was 'Mr. King',' said the reporter.

'We didn't,' said Motington. 'Not until Sullivan led us to this place. Then we guessed. You see, 'Mr. King' was only a rumour. We had no proof that he even existed. But we did know that Sullivan, Topp and Helman were responsible for the mailbag robbery and several other robberies, too, of which the proceeds were never recovered.'

'Was that little man, Larkin, in with them?' asked Michael.

Motington shook his head.

'He was one of our men,' he answered. 'He belonged to the Ghost Squad.' He explained what the Ghost Squad signified. 'In the course of his duties he must have stumbled on the fact that Sullivan and Topp were interested in this house, connected them with Crayle, and put two and two together . . . '

'So he did follow us that day,' said Michael. 'I suppose, when he heard Ann mention Bracken Cottage, he thought we were mixed up in the matter too.'

'We shall never know what he thought,' remarked the chief inspector.

'Sullivan and Topp went to a lot of trouble to ensure that the place would be empty so that they could search for the stuff, didn't they?' said Hoppy. 'Kidnapping Mr. and Mrs. Wayland . . . '

'I'm afraid we were a little lax there,' said Motington apologetically, 'though, actually, it would be more accurate to blame the fog. We lost sight of Sullivan and Topp. They gave the man who was tailing them the slip. It was due to this lady that we picked 'em up again.'

He looked across at the efficient Miss Biter.

'Miss Biter?' exclaimed Ann. 'How does she come into it?'

'You'd better tell them that,' remarked the chief inspector.

'I am employed by the Assurance Assessors,' replied Miss Biter. 'I suppose you would call me a private investigator.

They were anxious to recover the stolen property. It had cost them a lot of money, you see. I had the same idea as Chief Inspector Motington. I thought that Sullivan and Topp would eventually show me where the stuff was hidden.'

'That's why you took a job with us?' asked Ann.

Miss Biter nodded calmly.

'I saw your advert in the paper,' she replied, 'and it struck me as a good idea for being on the spot. Of course, I was working in with the police. You saw Sergeant Bishop signal to me that night, Mr. Wayland?'

'That was Sergeant Bishop, was it?' said Michael.

Again Miss Biter nodded.

'They had promised to have someone always near in case of trouble,' said the gaunt woman.

'Why couldn't you have told me?' demanded Michael.

Miss Biter looked slightly confused and the chief inspector laughed.

'She wasn't sure of you,' he answered. 'Neither were we, for that matter . . . '

'Surely,' exclaimed Ann indignantly, 'you didn't imagine that we had anything to do with it?'

'I said, we weren't sure,' replied Motington. 'You bought the house at a time that was most opportune — just after Sullivan was released. For all we knew to the contrary, you both might have been in it up to the eyes. And then, of course, there was the discovery of the dead body of Larkin in your loft . . . '

'You believed we had something to do with that, too?' cried Ann. 'Well . . . '

'The police usually suspect everybody connected with a case until they've proved that they're innocent,' said Motington. 'I'm beginning to believe that you and your husband can be given a clean sheet . . . '

'But you're not certain?' said Michael quickly.

'Very nearly, Mr. Wayland,' answered the chief inspector. 'Of course, you *could* have found the stolen property . . . '

'And had ourselves kidnapped and shut up in that beastly shed?' demanded Ann.

'It would have been a very good blind,'

murmured Motington.

'I can assure you it was nothing of the kind,' said Michael.

'I'm not suggesting it was,' said the chief inspector mildly. 'I only said it *might* have been.'

'Well, I hope you're quite satisfied about it,' grunted Michael. 'Where did you go on the night they got me?' he asked, turning to Miss Biter.

'I went over to Havershot with Sergeant Bishop to see Chief Inspector Bartram,' she replied. 'He drove me over and I got held up by the fog. When I did get back, the house was empty and I found a typed card saying that you and Mrs. Wayland had gone up to London. Of course, I knew that was all a fake . . . '

'I thought it was, too,' remarked Hoppy. 'But I couldn't be sure. Then when you turned up with that pistol . . . '

Miss Biter laughed. It was the first time they had ever seen her laugh and Michael thought it was ghastly.

'I came back to find a light in the house,' she said, 'and I thought Sullivan was there. I wasn't taking any chances . . . '

'What was the idea of leaving the house empty?' said Ann.

'We wanted to catch them in the act,' said Motington. 'Sullivan had taken the greatest pains to ensure that they wouldn't be interrupted. I think, if Miss Biter hadn't persuaded Mr. Hopkins to leave there would have been a great deal more trouble than there has been. Sullivan isn't squeamish and I don't suppose he'd have stuck at anything. Both you and your wife can consider yourselves very lucky people, Mr. Wayland. It might not have been only spending a few hours in a damp shed . . . '

'He must have typed that note,' murmured Hoppy.

'Yes. He knew you were coming back,' said Motington. 'He probably thought, if you didn't find Wayland and his wife here, you'd go back to London. That's why he held his hand until tonight.'

'Well, I'm very glad you've caught him,' said Ann. 'I shall sleep much happier knowing that dreadful man is locked up . . .'

But before she went to bed that night, Sergeant Bishop had returned with the news of Sullivan's escape.

14

Sullivan stumbled along the road in the fog, keeping to the narrow, muddy verge with difficulty. He would have liked to take a short cut to his destination across the field but he was afraid of getting lost.

That accident to the police car had been a bit of luck. He had been racking his brains how he could make a getaway, and had almost decided to risk a dash for it, when the skid had happened. That had been one piece of luck. If he'd worked things out right, he was in for another.

There was one thing about the fog, it offered ample cover. If it had been a clear night, he'd never have made it. They'd have been after him at once. But in the fog, they wouldn't know which way he'd gone. By the time it was clear, he'd be safe . . .

It was bitterly cold. He wished longingly that he'd got that bottle of whisky with him that he had stopped

Curly drinking too much from. The cringing, cowardly swine! Sucking up to the police. Curly had always been yellow — scared of anything, almost. He was glad he hadn't croaked him, though, in his fit of rage and disappointment. He wasn't worth it. He was probably locked up in a cell at Havershot police station by now, if they'd succeeded in getting him there. Well, let him rot there! Sullivan would have all the more for himself.

There was no sign of light yet, but the fog seemed to be getting a little thinner, Perhaps it was only just a patch. He hoped it wasn't going to clear — not before he'd reached his destination. They'd be out looking for him, and without the blanket of the fog . . .

He found a box of matches in his pocket, struck one, and looked at his watch. A quarter to four.

He felt very tired, and presently, finding a tree near the edge of the road, he sat down, resting his back against the trunk. The cold was striking right through him, but he must have a moment's rest.

There was no sign of life anywhere. He

hadn't seen a soul or a vehicle of any sort. Most people were still asleep in their beds . . .

He got up after about ten minutes and continued on his way. He still had quite a good distance to go. Well, it would be worth it when he got there. He'd be able to stay until the hue and cry died down, and then he could get right away — out of the country — with plenty of money and the prospect of a life of ease and luxury before him . . .

He'd have to be careful, though. There might be somebody else in the house other than the person he wanted to see. It would be no good knocking at the front door — not at this hour — and he dare not wait until it was daylight. Oh, well, he still had the screwdriver. There'd probably be a small window at the back that would yield to a little gentle persuasion . . .

He came at last to paved pavements as the open country gave place to the beginnings of a town. Dimly, through the thick mist, he could make out a row of shuttered shops and, farther on, houses.

The street lights shone blearily through the fog, small hazy circles of light that failed to reach very far.

He had no idea whereabouts the road lay that he was seeking. This was going to be his greatest difficulty. It would be easily missed, and he must find it before the daylight came . . .

The street he was in was evidently the main street. There were several turnings running off it, and Sullivan stopped to read the nameplate on each. No luck . . .

He walked on to the end of the main street. Which way now? The road he sought might be near or it might lie on the outskirts of the town. How was he going to find out?

He paused, uncertain what to do. There was nobody about to ask, even if he dared risk asking . . .

Better go on and hope for the best. He moved forward again. The mist was definitely thinning now. Houses that had been invisible began to loom up more and more clearly. Soon it would be daylight. He must find the place before that . . .

He came to another road. That wasn't

it. Surely he couldn't have passed it?

Ah, at last! There, in black letters on the white board at the beginning of the next road, was the name he wanted.

He turned into the quiet street, scanning the houses. This was the one. He entered the gate and walked quickly round to the back. The kitchen window — that would do . . .

The screwdriver was unnecessary. The window had not been latched. Cautiously and quietly, he pushed up the sash. A moment later, he was inside the house, enveloped in a comforting warmth.

He was safe.

They could search for him as much as they liked now, they'd never find him. Without a sound, he moved out of the kitchen and made his way to the hall. The dim staircase ran up into shadow. Softly, he went up until he came to a broad landing. There were two doors here, one on the right and one on the left.

Sullivan hesitated. Which was the door of the bedroom he wanted? He listened. There was no sound of any kind in the house. Very cautiously, he turned the handle and opened the door on the right. He could see nothing in the darkness of the room, but he could hear the sound of regular breathing. Someone lay asleep in the bed. Was it the person he wanted?

He crept forward in the direction of the faint sound. Dare he risk striking a match to make sure? Supposing it should be the wrong person . . . ?

He had to take the risk. With as little sound as possible, he took the box from his pocket, drew out a match and struck it. The tiny flame flared into life and he looked at the bed . . .

Mrs. Newsome stirred in her sleep and awoke.

'Don't make a sound or it'll be the worse for you,' hissed Sullivan.

She sat up in bed with a startled exclamation.

'Who are you? What are you doing here . . . ?'

'I'm Sullivan,' he said, and going to the door pressed down the light switch just as the match began to burn his fingers. 'I want the money and jewellery you took from the safe at Crayle's cottage . . . '

'I don't know what you're talking about — ' began the woman, but he cut her short.

'Oh, yes you do,' he broke in roughly. 'You're Crayle's sister. You knew all about the safe an' the money. After he was hanged you went to the cottage and cleaned out the safe . . . '

'You're talking absolute nonsense,' said Mrs. Newsome, looking at him steadily. 'I know nothing about it at all. If you don't go away, I shall call the police . . . '

'Will you?' snarled Sullivan. 'Supposing they insist on searching this house? What about that?'

Her eyes flickered for a second and he knew that he was right.

'All that stuff belongs to me,' he went on, 'and I'm going to have it . . . '

'Keep your voice down,' she said sharply. 'You'll wake my servant . . . '

'Servant?' he sneered. 'You're doing yourself pretty well on my money, aren't you?'

'We'll talk about that presently,' said Mrs. Newsome coolly. 'That money was the product of my brains, Sullivan. You and the other two only carried out my instructions.'

'You mean Crayle's,' said Sullivan, but she shook her head.

'I mean mine,' she said. 'My brother merely acted for me . . . '

Sullivan stared at her. This was something he hadn't expected. He had only thought that she had found the money and taken it . . .

'You are 'Mr. King'?' he asked.

She nodded.

'I am 'Mr. King',' she answered. 'Every robbery that you, and Helman, and Topp carried out was planned to the last detail by me.' She made a contemptuous gesture. 'My brother hadn't enough brains to plan anything. I conceived the whole scheme. I enjoyed it. If my fool of a brother hadn't bungled his part of it at the last, you wouldn't be standing there now.'

Sullivan's brows drew down in a puzzled frown.

'What do you mean by that?' he asked.

'You would have died like Lew Helman,' she said calmly. 'That was the intention — my intention. The mailbag robbery was to be the last. I have never believed in going too often to the well. Topp would have died in the same way. Perhaps William would have died too. I hadn't quite made up my mind about that, but a fool is always dangerous . . . '

Sullivan felt a sudden fear of this ugly woman with the beautiful voice. There was something so cool and inhuman about her.

'The original idea, as you were told, was that all the proceeds from these robberies should be retained until such time as it was safe to dispose of them,' went on Mrs. Newsome quietly. 'It was a safe plan. Most criminals are caught because they cannot exercise patience. They must spend what they have stolen at once, and so they give themselves away to the police. You three were sufficiently sensible to realize that it was safe. And, of course, you were told at the beginning that if you didn't adhere to the rules, word would be passed to the police that would be sufficient to convict you for any one of your offences.'

'Why are you telling me all this?' demanded Sullivan. 'I know it all. I'm not interested. I want my money.'

'I've said, we will discuss that later,' retorted Mrs. Newsome. 'I'm telling you what the arrangement was because I think it advisable. That was the arrangement as you knew it. You were, in addition, given a respectable sum of money after each operation — sufficient to keep you going comfortably but not sufficient to arouse the suspicions of the police. What you did not know was that I had other plans. I had no intention of sharing the proceeds with any of you. Starting with Helman, you were all three to be — eliminated.' She smiled and it was not a nice smile. 'Do I make myself clear?'

Sullivan swallowed hard and nodded. He was becoming desperately afraid of this woman in the bed.

'Unfortunately William bungled the first time, and it was the last, for him. I will say one thing in his favour, he was loyal. He said nothing.'

Sullivan clutched at the remnants of his remaining courage.

'Never mind all that,' he snarled. 'That's over and done with. I want money and I want hiding up. I managed to get away from the dicks . . . '

'And if you're caught they'll hang you,' said Mrs. Newsome, as though she were discussing the weather. 'You killed that man who was found in the loft.' She considered for a moment. 'Go downstairs,' she said, 'and wait for me. I will follow you in a few minutes.'

Sullivan obeyed. He went down to the kitchen and put on the kettle. His throat was dry and he still felt cold. What he wanted was a hot drink. There was no doubt that the woman upstairs had scared him. To coolly lie there and tell him that she had planned to have them all murdered when she had finished with them — it was ghastly. He was pretty tough himself but this . . .

In a few minutes Mrs. Newsome appeared. She had put on a padded housecoat and soft, dainty slippers.

'I see that you have put the kettle on,' she said. 'That was sensible. I'll make some tea.'

'*I'll* make it,' replied Sullivan, 'and I'll pour it out too.'

She laughed and there was genuine amusement in her eyes.

'Are you afraid that I'm planning to poison you?' she asked.

'I'm not taking any risks,' he grunted.

When the kettle was boiling, he made the tea, poured out two cups, and gave her one.

'Thank you,' she said. 'Now, we've got to decide what to do with you — '

'I'm staying here,' he broke in quickly.

'I know,' she answered, 'but I've got to account for you to my servant. She'll wonder, and she may talk. You don't want that, neither do I.'

She was silent, sipping her tea thoughtfully.

'There's a shed at the end of the garden,' she said, after a little while. 'You'd better go there. It's locked, but I'll give you the key . . . '

'I'll freeze,' he grumbled.

'It will only be for a short while,' she said. 'I'll make an excuse to send the woman away for a few days. By that time we can come to some other arrangement.'

'All right,' he said. 'What have you got in the way of food? I'm hungry.'

'There is some cold meat in the pantry,' she said. 'You'll have to be content with that. I don't want the smell of cooking filling the house.'

She got it for him, together with tomatoes, pickles, and bread. He ate ravenously. She looked at the watch on her wrist.

'It's nearly six,' she said. 'She'll be down at seven. Finish your tea, and go to the shed.'

He poured himself out another cup and gulped it down.

'Give me the key,' he said, 'and hurry up and get this woman out of the house. I want sleep.'

She fetched the key and opened the back door.

'There's the shed,' she said, pointing it out to him. 'You can lock the door on the inside.'

He grunted ungraciously, and she watched him go down the garden and disappear inside the small shed at the end.

Going inside again, she poured herself a second cup ot tea, and there was a smile on her lips as she drank it.

The situation had been unexpected, but she had, she thought, dealt with it adequately.

Sullivan would never come out of that shed alive . . .

15

By eight o'clock that morning with the exception of a few hazy wisps of vapour that clung to the hollows, it was quite clear, but there was a hard, white frost. Every bush and tree was rimed with glistening white. The garden and the woods beyond looked like a picture in a fairytale.

Michael and Ann were fast asleep. They had gone to bed almost immediately after Bishop had come to announce Sullivan's escape after the accident to the police car. Miss Biter had also gone to bed. But Hoppy felt restless. After Chief Inspector Motington had gone off with Bishop to assist in the search for the missing Sullivan, the reporter rambled about the sitting room, lighting Woodbine after Woodbine, his mind busily engaged in trying to puzzle out what had happened to the money and other valuables that had been in the safe.

It was obvious that the stuff had been kept there. It must have taken quite a lot of trouble and a good bit of ingenuity to install that safe in the chimney. It wouldn't have been put there for nothing. At some period or other the proceeds of the various robberies, carried out by Sullivan, Helman, and Topp, had been put there. When, and by whom, had the stuff been removed?

Had Crayle removed it before he was arrested for the murder of Lew Helman? It was possible, but it seemed unlikely. He hadn't expected to be caught. That had been the result of bad luck — if you could call it that. So it didn't seem a very plausible proposition to imagine that Crayle had removed the stuff. Also it was clear that Sullivan and Topp hadn't taken it. So who the dickens could have? Who else would have known, or suspected, that it was there? Could Yardle have found it? Was that the explanation for his sudden disappearance?

Hoppy shook his head.

It was almost impossible that he could

have found it by accident. If he'd had any inkling that the safe was there, he'd had years to get the stuff away . . . Perhaps that's what he had done. But then why leave it until now to disappear? No, Yardle didn't fit. Who else?

That sister of Crayle's. Could she have got it?

Hoppy had been aimlessly strolling about the room until this idea struck him. Now he stopped dead in his tracks. She could. She could have known that it was there. What was to prevent her, when the cottage was empty after her brother had been executed, coming along and removing the contents of the safe?

Hoppy was so forcibly struck with the plausibility of this idea that he decided to seek the help of Miss Biter. Braving that gaunt lady's displeasure, he ran upstairs and woke her up. At first she was considerably annoyed but, when she heard what he had to say, her annoyance was replaced by intense interest.

'I think you may be right,' she said. 'We'd better get in touch with Chief Inspector Motington, and tell him. Go down and wait for me. I won't be long.'

She was down in under two minutes, and the first thing that occurred to them both at almost the same moment was — how were they to get hold of Motington? Bishop had still got Michael's car.

It was solved by the efficient Miss Biter.

'I'll go on my bicycle to the nearest callbox,' she said. 'I can phone the police station at Havershot and get them to pick you up here.'

'What about you?' asked Hoppy.

'They can pick me up at the callbox,' said Miss Biter. 'I'll wait there for them.'

She was gone before he could argue.

It seemed an age to Hoppy before he heard the sound of a car coming down the road, and, going out to the iron gate, saw a police car with Miss Biter and Chief Inspector Motington on board. Miss Biter's decrepit bicycle was slung across the back. Waiting only to unfasten this, they set off for Camsford.

'It's rather a good idea of yours, I think,' said Motington. 'I wonder it didn't strike me. It's the logical conclusion, after all.'

'What are you going to do?' asked Hoppy. 'Supposing she denies all knowledge of the stuff?'

'I shall apply for a search warrant,' said the chief inspector. 'If she has got it, it's somewhere in the house. You can be sure of that. She wouldn't risk taking it anywhere else.'

The neat house in Roseacre Gardens, with its yellow-painted front door, looked the picture of prosperous respectability as they drew up at the closed gate. Was he right, thought Hoppy, as he got out of the police car, and waited for Miss Biter and Motington to join him on the pavement? Did this ordinary villa, in this ordinary road, conceal a vast fortune in stolen property?

They followed the chief inspector up the crazy-paved path between the rose bushes to the front door. Motington pressed the polished bell push.

There was a slight delay and then the woman, who had answered the door to

Michael when he had come to negotiate with Mrs. Newsome for Bracken Cottage, appeared.

'I should like to see Mrs. Newsome,' said the chief inspector.

The woman surveyed them without expression in her rather protruding pale eyes.

'Mrs. Newsome's in the garage,' she said.

'Would you tell her that Chief Inspector Motington would like a word with her?' said Motington. 'Or better still, we can go round to the garage . . . '

'I'll tell her,' said the woman.

She went away, leaving the door ajar.

'That's the garage round there,' said Hoppy, nodding to the closed doors, also painted yellow, that were set a few feet back from the front of the house.

'There's probably another entrance at the back,' said the chief inspector.

There was a longer delay this time, but eventually Mrs. Newsome came through from the back of the hall and looked at them inquiringly.

'You wish to see me?' she asked.

'Are you Mrs. Newsome?' said Motington, and she nodded. 'I would like to ask you a few questions.'

'You'd better come in,' she said, and led the way into the drawing room. 'What is it you wish to question me about?'

'It concerns Bracken Cottage,' said the chief inspector. 'Last night a safe was discovered behind the panelling over the fireplace in the main bedroom . . . '

He explained the circumstances.

'What has this to do with me?' inquired Mrs. Newsome when he had finished.

'Have you any knowledge of what happened to the contents of that safe?' asked Motington.

'I know nothing about it at all,' she replied. 'Why should you imagine that I do?'

'William Crayle was your brother,' said the chief inspector.

'He was, unfortunately,' she answered. 'But I knew nothing about his affairs. We were not even friendly. You tell me that there was a certain amount of stolen property in this safe. I was not aware of the fact. I was not even aware that such a safe existed. You are much better informed than I am.'

'You assert, positively,' said Motington, 'that you did not remove the contents of that safe after your brother's execution?'

'Certainly I do,' declared Mrs. Newsome. 'I've already told you that I was not aware of the safe's existence.'

'You would not object, then, to this house being searched?' said the chief inspector.

It was only a momentary flicker of alarm that came into her eyes then, but Hoppy saw it.

'I should object most strongly,' she said. 'Have you a search warrant?'

'No, but that could easily be obtained,' answered Motington. 'That is, of course, if you insist upon it. But if there is nothing here to find, why should you object to a search?'

'I object on principle,' said Mrs. Newsome.

'Very well,' said Motington, and his tone was slightly harder. 'I will obtain the warrant and come back. In the meanwhile, I must warn you that nothing is to be removed from the house, nor are you to leave it yourself.'

He turned to Hoppy and Miss Biter.

'I am leaving these people here,' he continued, 'to ensure that these orders are carried out. You are under no compulsion to allow them to remain inside the house, if you have any objection.'

In the depths of Mrs. Newsome's eyes there sparkled a glint of suppressed fury, but her voice was calm when she spoke.

'They can remain inside for all I care,' she said. 'I have met this young man before. I don't know the — other person.'

'This lady is employed by the Connaught Detective Agency,' said Motington smoothly. 'I shall return as soon as it is possible.'

Mrs. Newsome shrugged her thin shoulders.

'It's quite immaterial to me,' she said. 'I presume there is no objection to my continuing to polish my car?'

The chief inspector shook his head.

'So long as you remain on the premises,' he said and took his departure.

'Would you like some coffee?' asked

Mrs. Newsome, when he had gone. 'I usually have mine at this time.'

'No thank you,' said Miss Biter, and Hoppy declined too.

Mrs. Newsome left them. She went out into the kitchen, opened the back door, and made her way round to the garage. This, as Motington had suggested, had another door to it that opened into the garden at the back. Mrs. Newsome unlocked it and went inside, relocking it behind her.

She'd got to think, and think quickly. The coffee idea hadn't worked. For some time she had been taking sleeping capsules. A few of these dissolved in the coffee would have ensured that there would be no interruption from Hopkins and the woman. But they had refused the coffee. She had to do something. Once that policeman got back with his search warrant there would be trouble — bigger trouble than he imagined. She leaned against the bench that ran along one side of the garage, and frowned in concentration.

Everything had gone wrong. She had

felt so safe after all this time, and then Sullivan had appeared, and now this . . .

There was only one thing she could do. Get away.

That's what she must do — get away. It was her only chance . . .

From a drawer in the bench, she took out a round object of rubber. It was shaped like a cup and was attached to a stout wire. She moistened it under a tap in the corner, came back, and stooping under the bench, pressed the cup hard against the stone floor. The sucker adhered and she pulled with all her strength. Part of the floor came up like a trap, revealing an oblong compartment in the floor. In it was a stout, iron-bound box. The lid was fastened by a heavy padlock. She took a key from a chain around her neck and unlocked the padlock.

The box was full to the brim with notes and jewellery.

She took out thick packets of notes, piling them on the floor beside her. Then she closed the lid of the box, let down the stone floor, and removed the sucker, putting it back in the drawer.

Working swiftly, she transferred the packets of notes to the car. It was no use bothering with the jewellery. She would have to leave that. They could have it — if they could find it. It wasn't the contents of the hidden box that worried her. The stone fitted so well that she would have risked them overlooking it. It was the thing that was huddled up in the back of the car concealed by a rug . . .

She couldn't explain that away and there was no place she could hide it . . .

Her intention had been to dump it at the side of some lonely country road. There would have been nothing to connect her with it then. But that plan had been frustrated by the unexpected arrival of Chief Inspector Motington. There was still a chance, though, that she could get rid of it . . .

Her hat and coat lay on the driving seat of the car. She had brought them down, ready for her journey with the body. She put them on, and going over to the big double doors of the garage, quietly unfastened them . . .

The question was, how long a start could she count on? Those two in the drawing room would see her go, but they couldn't follow. They had no means of transport. Chief Inspector Motington had taken the police car. If she could get a reasonable start there might be a hope. Once she was away, the car would be more of a liability than an asset. She would have to abandon that at the first possible opportunity and travel the rest of the way on foot.

To where?

That was something she hadn't had time to decide. She would have to think of that after she had got away. She dare not delay too long or Motington would be back . . .

Gently she pushed the two doors open. There was no gate to the run-in to the garage, and she was thankful that she had not had one built, as she had intended. She would have a clear run to the road.

She got in the car, and settled herself behind the wheel. Her foot pressed on the starter and then at the second attempt the engine started into life. She moved the gear lever on the steering wheel and let in the clutch. The car moved forward . . .

Hoppy and Miss Biter heard the sudden sound of the engine, and the reporter ran to the window. He saw the car speed out of the garage and take a dangerous swing into the road.

'She's going,' he yelled to Miss Biter. 'She's going . . . '

'She's gone,' answered the gaunt woman bitterly. 'We ought to have guessed . . . '

But Hoppy wasn't listening. He dashed out of the room and tore open the front door, racing down the path to the gate. The car was almost at the end of the road. He looked quickly about him. A few yards up the street, a man was just getting out of a car that had drawn up outside one of the houses. Hoppy ran up to him, with Miss Biter who had followed him at his heels.

'I want your car,' panted Hoppy.

'You go to blazes,' said the astonished owner. 'I . . . '

Hoppy gave him a shove that sent him staggering back against the wall of a house, and jumped into the car. Miss Biter scrambled in beside him as he sent the car racing down the road at breakneck speed, the angry shouts of the man it belonged to following them.

Mrs. Newsome's car had turned the corner, but they caught sight of it a good way away in the distance, going away from the town. Hoppy set his teeth, and jammed his foot down hard on the accelerator. The car responded valiantly. The needle of the speed indicator shot round to forty, fifty, sixty . . . People on the pavements stopped to stare, but Hoppy wasn't interested. His eyes were on the car in front. Narrowly, he avoided a lorry laden with wood as it turned out of a side road, and went speeding on. Seventy. The car was rocking on the rough road, which had now taken the place of smooth macadam. But the car in front kept its lead.

In the driving mirror in front of her, Mrs. Newsome saw the car behind. She couldn't see who was at the wheel, but she was not going to take any risks. It was travelling at such an unusually high speed that it seemed it must be trying to overtake her. She dared not go any faster. The surface of the road was uneven. To put on more speed was courting disaster.

There was a side road approaching that would take her out into open country, skirting the woods that surrounded Bracken Cottage. If she could shake off the car behind long enough to give her the opportunity, she could run her car into the wood and leave it . . .

She had to slow down to turn into the side road, and the distance between the two cars decreased. She only just missed the hedge as she swung round the corner, but she straightened the car again and put down her foot.

As her speed increased, she looked in the mirror again. The other car was round the corner and coming along in her rear.

There was no doubt now. She was being followed. The car bounded and skidded among the deep ruts of the road she was traversing. It was very narrow, little more than a lane, but she knew that farther on it broadened as it ran alongside the woods.

If she could only get sufficiently ahead to keep out of the view of the driver . . . Just for a few minutes . . .

She increased her speed as the road came to a sharp bend, and, as she rounded it, she saw, too late, a huge tractor coming towards her and blocking the entire way.

She tried desperately to brake, but it was useless. With a crash of breaking glass, the car hit the tractor head-on. It bounced back, fell on its side, and lay, useless, with wheels still spinning, a crumpled mass of distorted and dented metal.

Hoppy, his face white, only succeeded in avoiding the wreck by an inch. As he brought the car to a screeching stop, the tractor driver came towards them.

'It weren't my fault, guv,' he cried. 'I couldn't 'ave done nuthin'. The car come round that there corner like a bludy bullet . . . '

Hoppy nodded. He went over to the wrecked car and looked in through the shattered window.

Mrs. Newsome, wedged in behind the

twisted steering-column, lay quite still. There was a great gash in her forehead from which the blood was running down her face . . .

Hoppy, with the assistance of the tractor driver, succeeded in getting the door open. He reached in and felt for the woman's heart.

'Is she dead?' asked Miss Biter at his elbow.

He nodded.

'Yes, I think so,' he answered.

16

'Well,' remarked Chief Inspector Motingham. 'After nearly seven years of work, we can write the case off as finished.'

'You never give up at the Yard, do you?' said Michael.

Motington shook his head.

'A case is never closed until it has been brought to a satisfactory conclusion,' he said. 'There are a lot of people who think we give up after a certain time, but we don't. We may not be able to move because of lack of evidence, but we're always hoping that that evidence will come into our hands. We're a very patient lot, you know.'

'And very persistent,' said Hoppy.

'You have to be,' said Motington. He took a sip of the whisky that Michael had poured out for him. 'It's a heartbreaking job, sometimes,'

'I'm sorry for poor Yardle,' said Michael. 'He had nothing at all to do with it . . . '

'That was sheer bad luck,' agreed the chief inspector. 'We got it all out of Curly Topp. He came here to look at the cottage, and saw the murder of Larkin. Sullivan had to kill him after that. We've recovered the body. In a disused tunnel on a closed railway line. Not a bad hiding place, when you come to think of it.'

'Why didn't they hide Larkin's body in the same place?' asked Hoppy.

'Topp says that was Sullivan's idea — to put it in the loft,' said Motington. 'He wanted the cottage empty. He thought the finding of a body in the loft would scare Mr. and Mrs. Wayland away.'

'Nothing will scare us away now,' said Ann. 'Not even the fact that I've probably got to do all the work in future.' She looked at Miss Biter. 'I suppose you wouldn't like to give up being a detective and stay here?' she asked.

Miss Biter shook her head.

'No thanks,' she said. 'But I may be able to help you. I know somebody who isn't very happy where she is. Actually she used to be one of our office cleaners, but took a job as cook-general. I think she'd like it here. I'll speak to her, if you like.'

'Would I like?' exclaimed Ann. 'I couldn't be grateful enough.'

'Did you get all the stolen stuff back?' asked Michael.

'Most of it,' said Motington. 'Some of the money had gone — a few thousand pounds — I suppose that's what she was living on . . . '

'I'd never have believed Mrs. Newsome capable of anything like that,' said Ann. 'I thought she was rather nice . . . '

'If she hadn't been killed in that crash, she'd have been hanged, like her brother,' said Motington grimly. 'Sullivan was dead when we found his body in the car. He'd been poisoned — a very strong dose of Barbitone. She had a lot of the stuff in her bedroom — in the form of sleeping capsules . . . '

'I suppose that's why she wanted to give us coffee,' said Hoppy.

Miss Biter sniffed.

'I wasn't falling for that one,' she said.

'She was in a nasty spot, you know,' said the chief inspector. 'She must have had the body of Sullivan in the house when we called.'

'There's a lot to be said for heredity,' remarked Michael. 'I wonder if there were any more in the Crayle family with the same kink?'

'They won't trouble us, if there were, darling,' said Ann. 'I'm going to concentrate in getting the garden just as I want it . . . '

'All this hasn't made you dislike the house?' said the chief inspector.

'I love it,' answered Ann. 'I can never be too grateful to that man at Camsford who told us to take the wrong turning . . . '

THE END

.1	41	61	81	101	121	141	16.
22	42	62	82	102	122	142	162
23	43	63	83	103	123	143	163
24	44	64	84	104	124	144	164
?5	45	65	85	105	125	145	16
6	46	66	86	106	126	146	
7	47	67	87	107	127	14	
8	48	68	88	108	128	1	
29	49	69	89	109	129		
30	50	70	90	110	130		
31	51	71	91	111	131		
32	52	72	92	112	132		
33	53	73	93	113	133		
34	54	74	94	114	134		
5	55	75	95	115	135		
6	56	76	96	116	136		
7	57	77	97	117	13		
8	58	78	98	118	1		
9	59	79	99	119			
0	60	80	100	120			

231	246	?61
232		
233		

F ... E

Gen ... Nazi
offic ... orces,
now ... Arab
heac ... oreign
Legio ... busi-
ness. ... nnaire
Texas ... ms to
captu ... face
justic ... imes.
In Tu ... ur ... rmer
had be ... espon ... ths of
thousa ... prisc ... d one of
them ha ... n Tex ... . .